GHOSTS OF AUTUMN

AMY GORDER

GHOSTS OF AUTUMN

BY

AMY GORDER

Bend, Oregon 2023

Emerald Books

Dedication

To Chris, my love and my light. Thank you, for .your constant support, encouragement, and great ideas.

To my four children, Meghan, Sarah, Erik, and Kelsey for many happy memories of reading books together. Those memories inspired me to write this book.

And to the ten young people who call me Nana: Aidan, Zachary, Owen, Hailey, Greer, Ava, Samuel, Bennett, Penelope, and Maisie, thank you for constantly reminding me that life is all about the adventure.

GHOSTS OF AUTUMN

II

"In the spirit world,
there is no time as we know it.
Past and future do not exist.
All 'time' is now."

—James Van Praagh

IV

1.

RYAN AND MATT

OCTOBER 1990

"Matt, I'm in!" Ryan yelled, waving to his best buddy from the other side of the broken window, high above. "Hurry!"

Ryan was tall for his eleven years and tan from hours in the summer sun. His chestnut hair was untidy, giving him the appearance of a wild child just returned from the jungle. He had a winning smile and the kind of face and easy way that people naturally gravitated toward. He was fearless and loved a good ghost story. Halloween was his favorite time of year, and ever since he was little, ghost stories of the Elk Grove Hotel intrigued him. He had never seen the decrepit building with his own eyes, but with talk of tearing it down, he felt the need to experience it himself. As usual, he asked Matt to tag along.

Matt had yet to catch up to Ryan's height. His hair was light, bleached by the sun, and he wore it short and undercut. His face was freckled and expressive, often in a state of uneasiness and apprehension. He was not one to enjoy stories about ghosts, flickering lights, or eerie organ music, and, aside from the candy, he didn't enjoy Halloween or anything to do with spirits and goblins.

He concealed his true feelings well, however, and secretly hoped Ryan would never know how afraid he truly was.

Matt assumed going to check out the Elk Grove Hotel was just another one of Ryan's "great adventures" and knew it would be easier to just go along with it. Matt sized up the old building: boarded windows below, broken windows above, crumbling bricks, rickety stairs, and one last wooden shutter hanging from a rusty hinge. A towering oak tree, its gnarly limbs twisting and turning, shouldered the building. He sighed and shimmied up the tree. Ryan waited with his hand out, grabbed Matt's hand, and pulled him through one of the window frames. Once inside, they eyed the room and all its contents, their mouths gaping.

"Hey, there's the organ I've heard about!" Ryan cried. "It's so cool!" He sat down on the bench and made a spooky face at Matt, which had the effect of a small smile, then pushed the ivory keys. No sound came.

"It's broken!" Matt grumbled, feeling less comfortable by the second. "Can we just go now?"

"Not yet! Let's go downstairs first!" Ryan ran from the room; Matt reluctantly followed. They creaked down the precarious stairs, both squinching their noses at the musty smell. Downstairs, tiny threads of light shone through boarded windows, barely enough for them to see, even after their eyes adjusted.

"There's so much cool stuff!" Ryan exclaimed, observing the odds and ends of furniture scattered throughout.

"More like junk," Matt groaned, knitting his brow. "Let's get outta here! We'll get in trouble if we get caught, and this place is creepy!"

"Calm down. We're not gonna get caught!" Ryan saw Matt's characteristic worry lines and backed off. "Just a little longer, okay?"

"No!" Matt shot back. "I'm leaving now. I'll wait for you by the window upstairs, and you better hurry up!"

Unfazed, Ryan continued down the hallway alone. Matt returned upstairs, keeping watch over his shoulder. He peeked into each room, before returning to the broken window. Time passed and his patience wore thin.

"Ryan?" he finally called. No response. "Hurry up!"

"Matt, come here!"

"Why?"

"Just do it!"

Ryan sounded different than usual, and Matt was too responsible to leave his friend behind, so against his better judgment, he descended the stairs for what he vowed would be the last time.

"Where are you?"

Ryan's voice quivered. "End of the hall."

In all his life, Matt had never been so frightened. Dappled golden lights and long shadows accompanied him down the corridor. He paused at the last doorway.

"Ryan?"

"Here."

He could see Ryan standing perfectly still, staring at something. He stepped in and saw what held Ryan's attention—a ghostly man, dressed in a miner's clothing, floated in the corner. The ghost was tall with bushy, rust-colored hair and piercing blue eyes. Matt moved next to Ryan, standing so close their shoulders touched. The spirit held out a large gold nugget, and flecks of light danced above it. The ghost stared at Ryan and then Matt, who was shivering. Ryan was spellbound, but Matt had seen enough. He grabbed Ryan by the arm.

"Let's *go*!" he cried, pulling him from the room. Ryan kept his eyes on the ghost.

A bright light followed them down the hall and up the stairs, washing over each room. Doors and shutters flew open and slammed shut again and again. The organ played, keys bobbing up and down, but there was no player.

Once at the window, Matt scrambled through and reached back to help his friend. But Ryan was frozen, mesmerized as he watched the organ roll slowly across the creaky wooden floor. It stopped before him. The spirit of a woman, dressed in blue, appeared. The ghost from downstairs stood beside her.

"Ryan, don't let them destroy our home," they said in unison, their voices loud and tinny. The man held out the gold nugget again, his eyes fixed on Ryan.

"Help us," the specter said.

"Ry!" Matt yelled from the window. "Come on!"

The ghosts vanished, leaving the organ silent in the center of the room. Ryan crawled out of the window and followed Matt down the oak tree.

"That was straight-up legit!" Ryan panted, still catching his breath. "Don't you think? The city wants to tear the place down! We can't let that happen!"

Matt was shocked. He turned sharply. "Are you crazy? It *should* be torn down! There are real ghosts in there! Ghosts who, by the way, knew *your* name!"

"Yes, but they didn't hurt us! All they did was ask for help! Aren't you a little curious about them?"

"No! And I want nothing more to do with this hotel!"

"But we could make a difference! Doesn't that *mean* something? We don't have to tell anyone we saw ghosts!"

"Whatever!" Matt yelled. "You're on your own this time! And if you tell anyone what happened here today, I swear I'll call it bogus. I want no part of ghosts, flickering lights, or stupid stuff like that! I'm done with you and your crazy adventures, Ryan!"

"Matt, wait! Please!" Ryan called, hoping Matt would turn back like he always did. But Matt was long gone, as was their friendship.

As he walked home alone, Matt knew the hotel had to go. And he vowed to make sure of it as soon as he had the power to do so.

Bob Thornton panning for gold on the Cosumnes River, 1851

2.
BIG BOB

OCTOBER 1851

Bob awoke to the sound of gunshots and yelling. He grabbed his pistol and slowly opened the flap of his canvas tent. Smoke from nearby campfires swirled with the morning mist, and the smell of bacon, coffee, and gunpowder filled the air. Two more prospectors paid a heavy price for their anger, and he could hear the wailing of their families. He waited for the noise to die down then crawled out, watching the area for more unwanted signs of trouble.

After stoking the coals from the previous night's fire, he warmed his hands and boiled a cup of cowboy coffee. Sipping from his tin cup, he looked over the Cosumnes River, watching the water snake its way through the blue oak and gray pine trees. The rising sun cast a rosy hue across the morning sky. When he finished his last drink, Bob wiped his mouth on his sleeve and untethered his mule, Sally, moving her to a new patch of grass. She nuzzled him and whinnied, then grazed.

This claim had produced only a few gold flakes in the past weeks, so Bob decided it was time to move on. He loaded the mule with his folded tent, meager supplies, and a few personal belongings. Then, waving his hat to other prospectors, he and Sally walked beyond the camp. A great blue heron spread her wings and squawked overhead. Bob paused and shaded his eyes with his hand, watching her soar then swoop to her nest in the deergrass along the river. This was just the sign he needed to renew his hope, and he was more determined than ever to return to Boston with enough money to prove to Jenny's parents he was worthy to marry their daughter.

Bob had known prejudice and poverty all his life. He was an Irish immigrant, orphaned at an early age and bullied by most everyone he met. He would have been destined to spend his life working morning to night on the docks and fishing boats in Boston Harbor, but he grew to be a strong, hard worker with initiative, and had taught himself to read and write. Most importantly, he had the determination to create a better life for himself.

On Sunday mornings, his only reprieve from work, he would walk the affluent Boston neighborhoods to see how others lived. He admired the large homes, fancy carriages, and people in their finery. And although he'd never been too religious, he found the churches, with their tall steeples rising to heaven, a peaceful place to sit and reflect.

On one of those mornings, he came upon a church with open doors. The sound of joyful organ music spilled out and drew him in. The music stirred him, but Bob was immediately transfixed by the talented and beautiful young woman playing the organ. Her lovely face was framed by dark barley curls, and she wore a long, blue dress. The moment Bob saw her, all his dreams came into focus. And that was how he first met Jenny.

She was everything he'd ever wanted, but she was from a wealthy family. She soon loved him, too, and didn't mind that he was poor. But he knew what a life of poverty meant. He also knew Jenny's family would never approve their marriage if he didn't have money. So, when he heard that gold had been discovered in California, he found a job on a clipper ship bound for San Francisco. Jenny cried when he left, handing him a small, brown poetry book, a token of her love. Bob swore he'd return as soon as he found his fortune.

Bob and Sally hiked along the riverbank, passing several encampments and a few lone tents, before coming to a deserted area where the river meandered south. The trees were bushy and thick, their canopies shining with autumn colors. Orange poppies with golden tips were scattered throughout the area. He smelled wild sage and noticed fish jumping in the river. It didn't take him long to decide this was the place he would stake his new claim.

Even though it appeared safe, Bob kept his hand close to his pistol. More stories had recently circulated throughout the camps of robberies and claim-jumping. It was believed that most of them were the handiwork of George and Cyrus Skinner, known throughout the Sacramento Valley as the Skinner brothers. Bob knew this was their territory, and they were bandits in the true sense of the word. More often than not, they would steal lives while also stealing gold, claims, and supplies.

With his boots still on, Bob waded into the shallow, dipped his pan into the silty soil, and raised it to swirl. As he did, a tiny flicker of light caught his eye. He peered at the light then rinsed and threw his pan to the shore and moved in for a closer look. There, wedged between two slate rocks, was a marble-sized gold nugget!

Alarmed by shaking in the trees, Bob drew his pistol from his holster and pulled back the hammer. A tule elk burst from the trees followed closely by a Miwok boy carrying a bow. The boy wore a buckskin breechcloth from his waist to his knees, no shirt, and had long black hair. He stopped when he saw Bob. Each was wary of the other, until the boy broke away and disappeared back into the trees.

Bob waited for a time, then slid his pistol back into his holster and brought the nugget up for a closer look. Could it be real gold? He bit the nugget to see if his teeth would leave a mark. Seeing the dint in the soft metal, he knew it was real and quickly stashed it in his pouch and scanned the rocks for more. Wedged lower was another nugget, a larger one, and below that, another. And between two more adjacent rocks were many more of various sizes. He had hit the Mother Lode! Still keeping a watchful eye, he raced to fill his pouch and pockets. No need to stake a claim now. He needed to get to the assayer in San Francisco as soon as possible!

3.
THE ELK GROVE HOTEL

OCTOBER 1851

The road was a flurry of activity that day, with 49ers heading to and from the goldfields and Sutter's Embarcadero. It was where prospectors would trade their gold for food, supplies, and services, including barbershops, restaurants, and saloons. Bob wasn't interested in those things. He just wanted to get to Sacramento, then on to San Francisco to weigh and trade his gold.

Bob had a kind way with people, which earned him a good reputation throughout the camps. He was well-respected by others, whether they actually knew him or not. Along the road, he would often be recognized, which wasn't hard due to his hair color and towering height.

"Howdy, Big Bob," they would say with enthusiasm as they passed. He would chuckle and politely respond. He wasn't sure who started calling him Big Bob first, but he didn't mind. He'd never had a nickname before.

He was surprised when one of the prospectors stopped him on the road. "Hey, Big Bob! Have you heard? The Skinner brothers are at it again!"

Bob frowned and shook his head.

"They've been on this road all day, just takin' things from folks, anything they can grab!" The man's eyes grew wider. "They shot a man earlier today. Not far from here. Took his supplies, everything! That fellow died!"

"Where were they last spotted?" Bob asked.

"A bit south of here, on the Monterey Trail."

No one but Sally knew the treasure Bob was hiding, and he intended to keep it that way. He said his goodbyes and hurried on. Ahead, a forked bolt of lightning struck, followed by an angry thunderbolt and blinding rain. Bob knew he needed to get off the road and certainly didn't want to come upon the Skinners in this weather or any weather, for that matter. He needed a safe place to stay and fast!

"Sir!" he yelled to a prospector headed in the opposite direction. "Do you know the nearest hotel?"

"Oh, hi there, Big Bob! Yeah, I passed one a mile back or so!" The man pointed, yelling over the loud downpour. "The Elk Grove Hotel."

"Thank you, much obliged." Bob hurried on as fast as Sally could go. If the Skinners came across him, they'd take everything, including his life, and he wasn't about to let that happen.

Still looking over his shoulder, he arrived at the new hotel just as the sun was setting and the rain was dying down. Two men, one older and gray-haired, the other, a younger version of the old man, ran from the stable.

"You lookin' to stay here tonight?" the older man called.

"Yeah, do you have room for my mule in the stable?"

"Of course." The man extended his hand to shake. "I'm James Hall, the owner, and this is my son, John. We'll feed and bed the mule while you check in. What's your name, sir?"

"Bob Thornton."

"Alright, then, Bob Thornton. My wife Sarah's inside. She's been playing the organ upstairs while the hotel's empty, so don't be alarmed. Just ring the bell on the desk between songs," he laughed.

Bob unpacked Sally and headed for the entrance of the impressive brick building. He stopped on the porch and glanced into the gloaming. Nothing alarmed him, so he turned his attention back to the hotel. Looking first through the glass side panel that adorned the cherrywood door, he entered, closing the door behind him. The comforting sound of the organ filled the air, and he couldn't help but smile. Closing his eyes, he pictured Jenny playing.

When the song was done, he tapped the brass bell on the counter and a woman with a cheery smile flew down the stairway to greet him. She was dressed in a plain brown frock, but her bright yellow apron warmed her dress and her smile even more.

"Hello, need a room?" she asked.

"Yes." Bob nodded, removing his hat. "You play the organ beautifully, ma'am."

"Thank you. It's one of the few belongings that made it here on the Overland."

"I'm sure it means a lot to you."

"It does. I can only play it when the hotel is empty of guests, and I do enjoy it. Now, how about you sign your name or make your mark here?" She pointed, sliding a worn ledger and an ink-well toward him. He signed his name and pushed it back. She glanced at the ledger.

"Nice to make your acquaintance, Mr. Thornton. I'm Mrs. Hall. You may have already met my husband, James, and our son, John, at the stable."

"Yes, I did." His brow furrowed. "I wonder, Mrs. Hall, have you had any trouble with thievery around here?"

"No," she said. "We've been lucky, I guess. I hear stories of those Skinner brothers all the time, though."

"Yes, well," Bob replied, "I heard they were on this road to-day, possibly headed toward Sacramento, but who knows? They might circle back. You might think about locking your doors."

"I suppose you're right. People can knock if they come in late. Which direction you headed?"

"Sacramento."

"Well, you be careful out there. Are you payin' with gold dust or money?"

"Gold dust."

"Okay, one pinch for the hotel, one for the stable, and another for breakfast, if you're interested." She held out a poke sack.

"Just the room and stable, ma'am." He paused. "Any chance I could be in the room with the organ? Reminds me of my girl. She plays, too." He reached into the pocket of his coat and pulled out a small, folded paper. He opened it, pinched what was left of the gold dust, and rubbed his fingers and thumb back and forth over the poke sack. When Mrs. Hall was satisfied that she had two full pinches, she handed him a brass-plated key.

"Your room's upstairs, Room 202, the room with the organ." She smiled and winked. "And watch your head going up those stairs. We don't have many guests as tall as you!"

"I appreciate that," he chuckled. "Thank you."

As Bob climbed the stairs, he heard the latch lock on the door below. Reassured, he walked down the hallway and opened Room 202. Dropping his belongings in the corner, he threw his hat and coat over a chair to dry and sat on the edge of the bed. Still not able to shake his fear of being followed, he pulled his Bowie knife from his boot and placed both the knife and pistol under the pillow, just in case he needed them quickly in the night.

Inspecting the room, he found the bed to be soft and certainly better than sleeping on the hard ground outside. He noticed the secretary's desk in the corner, noted the time on the clock, and sat down on the organ bench, gently touching the keys with his fingers. The presence of the organ was, to him, another sign his life was about to change.

Once settled in, he lit the oil lamp atop the highboy chest and got to work. After removing his damp red flannel shirt, he tore it into strips of various sizes and laid them on the bed. He searched Sally's side bags for a ball of twine he had tucked away, then emptied the nuggets onto the bed, thoughtfully arranging each one on a piece of flannel. He tore several small corners from Jenny's poetry book, rubbed them in the residue of the gold dust, wrapped each nugget together with a corner, and tied them tightly with the twine. He hid the bundles throughout the room in places he thought would not be easily discovered. The clock chimed the hour as he hid the last nugget, feeling confident no thieves, not even the Skinner brothers, would find the gold now.

Relieved, he opened the window and looked out over the dark hotel grounds. Rain was falling steadily. He heard a twig snap in the oak tree outside his window, but assumed it was caused by the wind. Finally, he sat down at the desk, opened his poetry book to an empty page, and wrote a note to Jenny.

My Dear Jenny,

I am staying at the Elk Grove Hotel in the new town of Elk Grove. I am returning the poetry book to you for safekeeping. Read between the lines.

Yours,
Bob

Then, further below, he wrote:

Mrs. Hall,

If something happens to me while I'm staying here, please send this poetry book and note to

Jenny Weatherly
210 Cambridge Street
Boston, Massachusetts

When finished, he tore the page from the book, folded it in half, and wrote Jenny's name across the paper. Tucking it loosely inside the book, he opened the cover to read Jenny's flowery handwriting one more time.

To Bob Thornton,

Come home to me soon!

Love, Jenny

Boston, 1849

Bob extinguished the light in the oil lamp and lay down, holding the poetry book close to his heart. He felt certain the gold was safe for the night and he would gather it and head to Sacramento in the morning.

"Jenny, I did it!" he whispered, then placed the book on the nightstand next to the bed. A cool breeze filled the room, and he drifted off to sleep, dreaming of Jenny and home.

4.
BANDITS!

OCTOBER 1851

Big Bob awoke to a loud thump. He sat up in bed and reached for the Bowie knife under his pillow. It was dark in the room, and he could barely make out the shadow of someone or something moving near the window. Another thud followed, much closer to him, and he recognized the sound to be the nightstand toppling over, spilling Bob's belongings, including the poetry book and the note.

"What's going on?" he asked, rubbing his eyes. "What do you want?"

"Where's the gold?" a deep, gravelly voice asked.

He didn't recognize the voice. "Tell me what you want," he said again, this time standing to his full height.

"Sit back down," a new voice growled, "and tell us where the gold is!"

Bob hid the handle of the Bowie knife in the palm of his large hand, the blade resting against his forearm. He figured he stood a chance if they didn't know he was armed or that there was a gun under his pillow. His eyes finally adjusted to the dark, and he was able to make out two distinct figures standing before him.

"We're not playing around," the taller shadow threatened. "Where's the gold?"

"What gold?" He tried to steady his voice.

The smaller shadow lurched forward, knocking Bob back on the bed and the shadow's knife appeared in Bob's face. "Listen carefully. We're not playin' around," he warned, spitting as he spoke. "Tell us where the gold is."

"I-I don't know what you're talking about," Bob stammered.

"Well, then, let me refresh your memory," the tall shadow replied. "You. Yesterday mornin'. The Cosumnes River. Lots of big gold nuggets." Then, bringing his face and his foul breath closer to Bob, he growled, "Is this ringin' a bell?"

"You must have mistaken me for someone else!"

"Are you Bob Thornton? Or, should I say, Big Bob Thornton?"

"Listen, I don't have any gold! I'm on my way to Sacramento to find work to pay my way home." Then he added, "Go ahead, look around the room. There's no gold here!"

While the smaller shadow continued to hold the knife to Bob's throat, the taller one looked through the furniture, opening and closing drawers, finding nothing. Angry and impatient, the shadow rummaged through Bob's bedding, throwing the pillow aside and sending Bob's pistol tumbling to the floor with a loud *thwack*.

Bob knew this was his only chance to escape. He raised the Bowie knife and thrust it at the man's chest. The shadow collapsed on the bed, moaned, and fell silent. The next sound was a single gunshot.

Planning to exit through the window onto the balcony and down the oak tree, the remaining shadow was forced to change his plans when two armed men ran out the front door of the hotel. The bandit had taken a chance and jumped from the upstairs balcony, landing hard on the ground below. He tried desperately to crawl away, but the searing pain from his injury was too much and he didn't get far.

"Stop right there!" Mr. Hall cried as his son pulled back the trigger of his shotgun. Mr. Hall kicked the man's gun out of reach and dragged him up the steps and through the lobby to the dining room, where he was tied up until the sheriff could arrive from Sacramento.

"What's your name?" Mr. Hall asked, before placing the gag over his mouth. The man growled defiantly, refusing to answer. "That's alright," Mr. Hall said, pulling the gag as tight as he could. "I suspect the sheriff will know you."

Upstairs, Mrs. Hall opened the door and entered Room 202. She gasped at the horrible sight of two men lying still and silent on the bed. One a stranger, the other their guest. Tears spilled on her apron as she wept over the lifeless body of Big Bob Thornton.

GHOSTS OF AUTUMN

5.
THE SCENE OF THE CRIME

OCTOBER 1851

Sheriff Joseph McKinney arrived in Elk Grove two days after receiving a letter from James Hall stating that two murders had taken place at the Elk Grove Hotel. Two men, he wrote, had broken into a hotel room with the intention of robbing the guest. During the attempted robbery, one of the intruders had been killed, as well as the hotel guest, and the third man was apprehended when he tried to escape. Mr. Hall wrote that the third man was being held in his custody and had refused to give his name.

The road from Sacramento to Elk Grove was busy that day, and the weather was unseasonably warm for the month of October. Sheriff McKinney rode his horse, Chester, up to the stable and dismounted. He watered his horse before taking a drink himself and pulled the heavy saddle from Chester's back.

The door of the hotel swung open, and the Halls walked briskly across the lawn to greet him.

"Welcome, Sheriff!" Mr. Hall cried out. "Boy, are we glad to see you!"

Sheriff McKinney removed his low-crowned hat and nodded. He was a young man, lanky and dark-haired, bearing a wiry mustache. He wore a tin badge on his black leather vest, and in his gun holster was a Colt Revolver.

"Howdy do," he replied, extending his hand to Mr. Hall. "Now, where's the prisoner?"

"He was tied up in the dining room, but when the hotel got busy, we moved him to the kitchen lean-to."

"His leg is badly injured," Mrs. Hall added. "I've tried to care for it, but it doesn't look good."

Mr. Hall waved the sheriff toward him. "This way, Sheriff. I'll take you to him."

Sheriff McKinney followed the Halls through the hotel and into the lean-to. The prisoner sat on a chair in the corner, his hands tied behind his back, the kerchief gag tightly covering his mouth. He was dirty and sweaty, and reeked of disease and smoke. His pants were torn and bloody. The sheriff took one look and recognized him.

"Well, well, well," the sheriff began, "as I live and breathe. If it ain't George Skinner."

George made a feeble attempt to speak through the kerchief. The sheriff shook his head.

"Now, now, this is most certainly not a good time to try to defend yourself, George. I'm sure you understand."

Sheriff McKinney rubbed his chin. "I've been hearing stories, George. In fact, many stories recently. It seems you and Cyrus like to shake things up on the Monterey Trail."

The prisoner attempted to speak again, and the sheriff held up his hand. "I wasn't expectin' a real answer, George."

"Mr. and Mrs. Hall, can you please tell me what happened?"

Mr. Hall cleared his throat. "Well, we—that is, my family and me—heard a gunshot in the middle of the night. So, John and I grabbed our guns and ran out the front door to see what was goin' on."

"Exactly what did you see, Mr. Hall?" the sheriff asked, still eyeing George.

"Well, Sheriff, we saw this fellow here on the second-floor balcony. He was headed for the oak tree. I guess he was fixin' to climb down. Anyway, when he saw us with our guns, he jumped. Broke his leg, but still tried to crawl away. That's when we grabbed him and tied him up and sent you the letter that same morning."

The sheriff shook his head up and down slowly. "I see. And what about you, ma'am?" he asked. "Do you have anything to add?"

"We only had one guest that night, Sheriff. His name was Bob Thornton. Real nice fellow. He was staying in Room 202 upstairs. When I heard the commotion outside, I ran and got the key and when I opened the door, I saw Bob and another man layin' across the bed. They were both long gone."

Sheriff McKinney nodded, then removed the gag from George's mouth.

"Now, don't talk unless I ask you to," he warned, pointing his finger close to George's nose. "I'm in a pickle here. I've given you more chances than the quills on a porcupine."

The sheriff clicked his tongue and shook his head. "This criminal livin' has finally caught up with Cyrus, and—" He pointed to

George's badly broken leg. "It looks as though it's caught up with you, too."

The sheriff walked across the room, picked up a chair, and set it down across from George. He lowered himself and leaned back with his legs outstretched, pushing up his hat.

"Tell me, George, what exactly were you boys up to in Room 202 that night?" He motioned. "You can speak now."

"Well, Cy was lookin' to rob someone, and he knew that man had found gold, so we followed him and waited until the lights went out. I didn't want to. I kept sayin', 'Cy, let's just go! Let's not look for no trouble.' I didn't want no trouble, Sheriff, but Cy, he wouldn't hear of it. 'George,' he said, 'we're climbin' that oak tree into that window.' And you know what Cy was like, Sheriff. He was my older brother, and he was mean, so I couldn't say no. He made me do it. So, we climbed in the window, and we asked that man where the gold was." George looked like a scared rabbit.

"Okay," the sheriff shrugged, "what happened next?"

"Well, we looked for the gold in the room, but couldn't find nothin'. And we didn't know he had a knife in his hand. And then, when I heard the moans comin' from Cy, I knew he was stabbed and done for, and that man had to pay because Cy was my brother. I didn't want to, but I had to, Sheriff. You understand, I'm sure. So, I took care of it and left right quick."

The sheriff glanced over at Mr. and Mrs. Hall. "Do either of you have anything to add?"

Mrs. Hall looked down and was silent. Mr. Hall said, "No."

The sheriff turned back to George. "So, let me get this straight. You didn't find any gold?" George shook his head.

The sheriff turned to the Halls. "And neither of you found any gold ? Is that correct?"

"No gold," Mrs. Hall answered, "but you're free to look again if you want. I put all the guest's belongings in a trunk and made sure no one stayed in that room until you got here, Sheriff."

"Thank you, ma'am. I'm much obliged."

The sheriff stared at George for a long time, then drew in a deep breath and blew out a long whistle. "Well, no one can accuse you of being the smartest person in the room, and that's for sure." George looked confused.

"Mr. Hall, you got a sturdy rope in the stable I can use? If you do, please go get it. George and I will meet you out front under the oak tree. Looks like we got us a hangin' to do."

GHOSTS OF AUTUMN

6.
JENNY

OCTOBER 1852

Jenny stepped off the stagecoach and found herself captivated by the sight of the Elk Grove Hotel and Stage Stop. She eyed every corner, amazed at how lovely it was: golden leaves fluttering in the trees, overgrown green grass swaying in the breeze, and yellow chrysanthemums outlining the porch.

"Here you go, ma'am," the driver called from above, handing down a floral carpet bag.

"Thank you." She smiled and strolled toward the entrance, holding the handrail as she ascended the steps.

The driver pulled a blue leather trunk from the boot of the stagecoach and placed it next to the entry door.

"Anything else I can do for you, ma'am?" he asked, removing his hat. He was obviously fond of this delicate young woman who was so far from home.

"No, I think I'll be fine now. Thank you, Charlie." She coughed into her handkerchief.

Charlie nodded and replaced his hat. Jenny watched as he leapt to the whip of the stage, snapped the reins, and whistled to the horses. When she could no longer see the coach in the distance, she opened the door and stepped inside, pausing to view the portraits in the hallway.

They must be the owners and their children, she thought.

"Hello, Miss," a voice called from across the room. "Or is it missus?" The woman winked, her long skirt waving as she briskly walked behind the lobby desk. Jenny recognized her from the portraits.

"It's miss," she answered politely. "Jenny Weatherly."

"I'm Sarah Hall. Welcome to the Elk Grove Hotel." She slid the ledger across the desk. "Your perfume sure smells nice! Roses, is it?"

"Yes, thank you. It was a gift from someone very dear. I wear it every day."

"It's lovely. I haven't worn perfume for years! Not much call for it out here." Jenny passed the ledger back.

"So, what brings you to Elk Grove, Jenny? You don't mind if I call you by your first name, do you?"

Jenny shook her head. "Heavens, no. I don't mind at all."

"Then you may call me Sarah."

Jenny's light expression turned serious. "Actually, I'm here because I'm looking for someone. My fiancé. His name's Bob. We're from Boston, and he came to California hoping to strike gold." Her eyes filled with tears. "The last letter I received was well over a year ago. He told me news of California and his experiences panning for gold in the camps. He said he was tired of sleeping on the ground and thought a real bed sounded nice. That was the last I ever heard, and that wasn't like him. So, I thought I'd start my search here, the closest hotel to where he was. Do you remember a tall man with red hair named Bob?"

Jenny coughed and Sarah noticed a tinge of blood appear on the handkerchief. Her heart sank for this young woman who was obviously in poor health. Her skin was sallow and her lips bright red. The gray circles beneath her eyes belied her attempt to appear well. She looked tired and frail. Sarah's motherly instinct told her Jenny needed her care.

"Jenny," Sarah said tenderly, "what was Bob's last name?"

"Thornton," she replied, her eyes searching Sarah's face.

Sarah stepped out from behind the desk. "Dear, let's go to the dining room and have a nice hot cup of tea. You've had a very long trip, and tea is always good for the soul."

Jenny nodded gratefully, coughed into a fresh handkerchief, then picked up her carpet bag and followed Sarah to the empty dining room. Sarah poured hot tea while Jenny sat and gazed out the nearby window.

James came bustling in through the back door of the dining room just as Sarah placed the steeping cups of tea on the table. His arms were full of sugar pumpkins that he carefully laid atop an empty table.

"James," Sarah said, "let me introduce you to our new guest, Jenny Weatherly."

James could tell from the tone in Sarah's voice that something was off.

"Nice to meet you, ma'am," he smiled, then turned to his wife. "Looks like we have enough pumpkins for several pies!"

"Yes, I suppose we do." A worried look washed over Sarah's face. "James, Jenny has come all the way from Boston looking for someone who's missing. She's trying to locate her fiancé, Bob Thornton."

"B-Bob Thornton?" James stammered awkwardly and sat down.

Sarah placed her hand on Jenny's. "Jenny, Bob was here."

Jenny looked deep into Sarah's eyes and then to James.

He anxiously ran his hand over his gray beard. "You see, Jenny, Bob was on his way to Sacramento. He checked in here for the night. The rumors are that he had discovered gold and was making his way back to Boston. The gold was never found, though." He hesitated and looked at his wife.

Mrs. Hall took a deep breath. "The night Bob stayed here, two men broke into his room looking for gold. A fight broke out and two people were killed." Sarah closed her eyes, not wanting to break the news. "I'm so sorry, Jenny, but one of them was Bob."

Jenny lowered her head and wept. It was obvious that her heart was broken. "I was afraid of this."

They sat for a while, Sarah patting Jenny's hand.

"Did he leave anything behind?" she finally had the strength to ask.

Sarah turned to James. "Can you bring the trunk with his things?"

James left the room and returned shortly. "We saved these just in case someone came looking." He placed the trunk on the floor beside Jenny and propped open the lid.

Slowly, she pulled each item from the trunk, her tears spilling onto Bob's hat, his flannel shirt, a pair of trousers, his boots. At the bottom of the trunk were his saddle bags and miner's supplies, and below, a Bowie knife and pistol. She left the knife and pistol, not touching them.

"Do either of you remember a poetry book? It was brown and pocket-sized, my gift to him before he left Boston."

"I don't remember it," Sarah said, shaking her head. "There were books thrown about during the scuffle, but I don't recall seeing a small brown one."

Jenny looked to James. "I'm sorry, no."

She coughed again, the coughing made worse from crying.

"Jenny," Sarah offered, "would you like to go up to your room now and rest? You must be very tired." Jenny nodded.

They walked together, arm in arm, up the stairway to Room 202. "This was Bob's room," Sarah said, then embraced Jenny and closed the door, leaving her alone with her thoughts.

Jenny sat on the edge of the soft bed and glanced around the room, her eyes landing on the organ. She smiled through her tears. So many memories of playing the organ for Bob, who would watch her with pride from across the parlor.

She opened the window and looked over the hotel grounds, imagining Bob gazing out at the same view. Somehow in that moment, she felt as close to him as she had ever been. It was as if he was standing beside her.

Exhausted by the long trip and the sorrowful news, Jenny lay down on the bed, placed her head on the soft downy pillow, and felt herself drift off. She dreamed Bob was running toward her carrying a bouquet of blue forget-me-nots. He waved and called her name. *"Jenny! Jenny!"* She was well and strong again. She ran to meet him, and they embraced and laughed and were happy!

Jenny died peacefully in her sleep that night, with Bob beside her.

*Jenny arriving at the Elk Grove Hotel
by stagecoach, 1851*

7.
MR. KELLY

OCTOBER, PRESENT DAY

Mr. Ryan Kelly was a popular history teacher at Pioneer Jr. High. He was approachable, fair, and had a knack for engaging his students and opening their minds to new ideas. The morning bell rang, and he opened the door and high-fived or fist-bumped each kid.

Running his hands through his tousled hair and smoothing his gold paisley tie, he waited for the morning commotion to settle and his students to take their seats.

"Alright, everyone. Today I'm going to tell you a story." Mr. Kelly never began lessons this way, which immediately grabbed Zoey, Amelia, and TJ's attention.

"So, a long time ago..."

"In a galaxy far, far away?" Zoey beamed. She was fun to have in class. She created many opportunities for laughter, and even Mr. Kelly couldn't help but chuckle at her jokes. She was small with bouncy, dark curls and a collection of basketball jerseys she wore with pride.

"No, not *that* far away!" Mr. Kelly exclaimed. "In fact, not far at all! There was a time when Elk Grove wasn't even a town, much less a city. Can you imagine what it was like without the people, buildings, or traffic here?

"When James Marshall discovered gold in the American River in 1848 and took his discovery to John Sutter, California changed forever. The land we're on now was mostly inhabited by the Miwok Indian Tribe. When gold was discovered, people came from all over the world to find their fortunes. James and Sarah Hall, along with their five children, were among those who traveled west in 1850 on the Overland Trail." He pulled down a map of the United States and traced the trail.

"But the Halls weren't looking for gold. They were looking to make their fortune in a different way. They came here to build a hotel where the 49ers and other travelers could stay. So, they built the Elk Grove Hotel and Stage Stop, and the town of Elk Grove was born."

"Why here?" Amelia asked. "Why not build a hotel where it was more populated?" She was an honors student who was widely respected by her peers. She was humble, too, and didn't hesitate to smile, despite her mouthful of braces. She wore her long, sandy brown hair pulled back in a ponytail.

"Good question," Mr. Kelly replied, pointing to the map again. "The Halls built the hotel here because of its proximity to the Monterey Trail, which ran north and south, connecting Monterey, the old Mexican capital, to Sutter's Fort in Sacramento. It was also a desirable location for the 49ers who traveled east and west between Sutter's Embarcadero, which we now call Old Sacramento, and the goldfields of eastern California and the Sierra Nevada. So, there was a good amount of traffic here as well."

"That was smart," TJ interjected, side-swiping his hair. TJ's real name was Theodore Joseph, which was shortened to TJ early on. He loved a challenge more than anything and was always up for adventure.

"Yes, it was very smart," Mr. Kelly agreed, "and more people actually made their fortunes through goods and services than through gold prospecting. And the hotel was something to see! The newspapers described it as a two-story brick building with a stately cherrywood entry and a wide front porch with rocking chairs. Inside, guests would sign in at a modern lobby desk, and down the hall was a dining room, kitchen, and saloon. Upstairs was a large ballroom and guest rooms, complete with a balcony. It was something!"

"Who named Elk Grove?" Amelia asked.

"Well, we don't know for sure, but some believe Mr. Hall named the town after finding elk horns in a grove of trees nearby. We do know that when the building was completed, Mr. Hall painted a sign with an elk's head, hung it over the entry door, and the town would forever be known as Elk Grove."

Mr. Kelly projected an image of the hotel onto the whiteboard. "The hotel earned a great reputation. For the right price, a traveler could rent a room, enjoy a home-cooked meal, even take a bath. But services and supplies were expensive, and a hot bath back then would cost them equal to $165 today!" The students were shocked.

"They paid that much to take a bath?" Zoey asked, crinkling her nose. The class broke into laughter.

"Yes, lots of people were willing to pay that much, especially if they hadn't had a bath in months, even years!"

"Mr. Kelly," Sophia said, tying her pink-tipped hair up into a messy bun, "I've seen the Elk Grove Hotel and, I can tell you, it's a scary-looking place!"

Sophia had attended school with Amelia, TJ, and Zoey since kindergarten. Even though they were often in the same class and lived in the same neighborhood, they had never been close friends. A "hi" in the hallway was the closest they came. Mostly this was due to different interests. Sophia loved to dance and paint and had a special fondness for photography, while TJ, Amelia, and Zoey liked sports and outdoor games. Sometimes they had differing opinions in class, which seemed to stem from their parents' opinions. But Mr. Kelly had established firm boundaries for discussions, so they accepted each other's differences and left it at that.

"People say the hotel is haunted, too!" TJ added.

"It's not haunted. It's just scary-looking and run down," Sophia replied.

"I don't know," TJ said, shaking his head. "I've heard a lot of rumors."

"Yes, there *are* many rumors," Mr. Kelly agreed. "Let's take a minute to name them. What have you heard?'

TJ shrugged. "There's no electricity, but lights turn on and off."

"Okay," Mr. Kelly said, "what else?"

"Shadows of people in the windows, maybe ghosts," Amelia said.

"Organ music, but no one knows who's playing it?" Zoey added.

"Right," Mr. Kelly nodded, "but do any of you know what happened at the hotel in October of 1851?" He waited. The class was silent. "Have you ever heard the name Big Bob Thornton?" No one replied.

"Big Bob was rumored to have discovered a bounty of gold nuggets while panning the Cosumnes River, not far from here." He pointed to the river on the map. "He stopped for the night at the Elk Grove Hotel, and while he was sleeping, two notorious bandits, George and Cyrus Skinner, climbed in through his open window. There was a scuffle, and Bob was shot and killed."

All eyes were glued to their teacher, who now circulated throughout the room.

"Now, that's a tragic story, but there's more. The gold was *never* found. The Hall family looked for it. The sheriff, Joseph McKinney, looked for it, and for years, others have looked for it, but *no one* has found it! Was the gold just another rumor?" he shrugged. "Or was it true?"

Amelia raised her hand. "I heard the city council wants to tear down the hotel."

"Yeah, to build another golf course," TJ said. "My parents don't want that. They support saving the hotel."

Mr. Kelly returned to the front of the room. "You're both right. This attempt to tear it down has been going on for years. If it weren't for the Elk Grove Historical Society, it would be long gone." He glanced around the room. "Would any of you like to share your thoughts on that?"

"I think the golf course makes sense," Sophia replied. "I mean, what's the point of keeping that old hotel around? My parents think a golf course would be better for the town."

"Okay, but what if the hotel could be restored and possibly made into a museum? What then?" Mr. Kelly asked. "What if the Elk Grove Historical Society had enough money to do that?"

"Wouldn't a golf course still make more sense?" Sophia asked.

"A museum where people could learn about the Gold Rush history of our town would make more sense," Zoey replied. Sophia looked skeptical.

"Different opinions," Mr. Kelly noted, "and that's what the city council is trying to figure out now. The Elk Grove Historical Society has been working to raise enough money to preserve this historical landmark, but they're still falling short."

"What's your opinion, Mr. Kelly?" Sophia asked. "Are you a member of the historical society?"

"I am, but I realize not everyone agrees."

His memory of racing through the hotel with Matt flashed through his mind. Matt had been terrified. Even as children, Ryan Kelly and Matt Fox couldn't agree on the hotel, and now that Matt was mayor, he had the power to push through the golf course. As president of the historical society, Ryan had his work cut out. The money hadn't been easy to raise, despite the town's support, and Matt might be impossible to convince.

"There will be a public council meeting to discuss the future of the hotel soon," Mr. Kelly said. "It will be an open forum, so perhaps some of you would like to voice your opinions before the council. I'll hand out the details later today."

"My parents say the hotel is a goner," Sophia scoffed. She placed her hands in her gray hoodie pocket.

"Not necessarily," Amelia replied. "There's tons of support for the hotel!" She turned back to Mr. Kelly. "Is there anything we can do to help save the hotel?"

He brightened. "Well, recently, the historical society hired an architectural firm to inspect the hotel, and they found it to be sound. That means the structure of the building is good and it can be safely restored. There still isn't enough money to refurbish the building, though, so we're going to begin with the basics while we continue fundraising.

"This Saturday, there's going to be a work party at the hotel. We're going to clear the grounds of debris and trim, weed, and prune the bushes and hold a volunteer picnic after the rummage sale. Lots of hands make light work, so if any of you would like to help, you will be welcome. In fact, I'll make this an extra credit assignment for those of you who want to participate."

Amelia, Zoey, TJ, and others agreed to be there.

Sophia thought it was probably a waste of time, but needed the extra credit, especially after that last history test, so she agreed as well.

GHOSTS OF AUTUMN

42

8.
MATT FOX

Mayor Matt Fox parked his shiny new pickup at the edge of Elk Grove Park. After adjusting his sunglasses and his orange Fox Construction cap, he drank the last sip of coffee, locked the door behind him, and headed across the park to the lone pathway leading to the hotel.

After years of working at his parents' construction company, Matt had recently taken over when they retired. Shortly thereafter, he launched a campaign for mayor and won. Networking proved to be profitable, and Matt knew money would pour in when his company built the new golf course. To make it work, though, he needed the land where the hotel now stood. If the hotel was razed, the city would approve it, and construction would commence.

Amelia, Zoey, and TJ were helping load gardening tools into wheelbarrows. Sophia stopped to pitch in when she realized they needed more help. Her older brother, Chase, and his best friend, Hunter, both former students of Mr. Kelly's, walked past, engaged in a lively discussion about Chase's new skateboard. They only showed up for the hot dogs Mr. Kelly had promised.

"Hey, Mayor!" Chase called. "Instead of a golf course, why not build a skatepark?"

"That would be sick!" Hunter added, high-fiving Chase.

Matt raised his hand to acknowledge them but made no attempt to stop or respond. He was on a mission to find Ryan Kelly.

Once on the path, the sights and smells of the woods transported him back to childhood. So many fond memories of playing, bike riding, and exploring with Ryan. As the path turned, the hotel came into view, much of it shrouded by a wall of overgrown shrubs. Dense oak and sycamore trees drooped around it. Yellow caution tape lay on the ground, an obvious sign the warning had been ignored. Matt looked up at the towering building. It was just what he expected to see after twenty years: rundown, porch caving, steps sagging. The sight of it made him jittery.

Volunteers gathered at the front steps. Ryan would take the lead; Matt maintained his distance.

"Thank you, everyone, for coming!" said Ryan. "As you can see, there's a lot of work to be done before our barbeque later today and our picnic after the rummage sale next week. The good news is with every rummage sale, we get closer to our goal of preserving this beauty!" Some clapped and others chuckled. "The trees will be taken care of by an arborist, so for now, let's just focus on pruning bushes, raking debris, and picking up trash. Any questions?"

Only Hunter raised his hand. "What time is the cookout?"

"Later, after our work here is done," Ryan replied. Hunter groaned.

Ryan spotted Matt in the back and waited for the crowd to disperse.

"Hello." Ryan reached out his hand. Matt hesitated, then returned the gesture. "It's been a minute."

"Ryan." He nodded, not making eye contact. "I'm not here to make small talk."

"Okay…uh, what brings you here? Are you volunteering?"

"Hardly," Matt scoffed. "What exactly is this? Saving the hotel again? Eventually, you've got to give it up and do what's best for the community."

"Yeah, but I'm not about to give up yet. Most people I've talked to are in favor of saving the hotel."

When Ryan and Matt were boys, the city council had campaigned to raze the hotel and replace it with a swimming pool. The citizens had overwhelmingly opposed the proposal, and it was dropped. A few years later, the council proposed replacing it with a public pool again. As a high schooler, Ryan had been instrumental in stopping this by rallying supporters and organizing protests.

This time, the call was for a new golf course, which had more support than the public pool ever did. Ryan was sure he could still find the backing to keep the historic hotel from destruction, but everything rested on the historical society's ability to raise enough money.

Matt shook his head. "I don't understand why this means so much to you."

"Well, first of all, a museum of Elk Grove history would benefit my students. Secondly, I think you know the answer."

Matt ignored the last comment. "A museum could be anywhere in town, man!"

"But it wouldn't be the very first building in Elk Grove! It's where the town was born! And I believe the majority of our citizens still support it. Besides, a golf course could be built anywhere, too."

Matt scoffed. "The golf course is coming, Ryan. Prepare yourself. One more public meeting, and the council will be ready to pull the trigger."

Ryan gave up. "Look, could you just pump the brakes and give us a little longer? For old times' sake? The historical society is working hard on fundraising. We think we'll have enough money to begin refurbishing soon."

"Oh, please!" Matt chuckled. "The hotel is a lost cause. I'm sure you're not even close to having the money! Besides, how do you know the building's even viable?" In his head he thought, *Not to mention the ghosts inside.*

"We know because we hired an architect who found the structural damage to be minimal and the foundation to be stable. We can do this! Have a little faith. Please."

Their eyes fixed on each other.

"Look," Matt sighed, "nothing good can come from saving this building and the land can be put to better use. It's my job to do what's best for the community."

"No, Matt. You're thinking in dollar signs. Everyone knows building a golf course would line your pockets nicely."

Matt's expression turned to anger. "It's time you stopped being a dreamer!"

"And it's time you stopped fearing the hotel!"

Matt turned away from Ryan, scanning the work party now in full swing. There were more volunteers than he expected. *Could Ryan be right?* he wondered.

Elections were coming, and he needed another four years to accomplish his goal of razing the hotel. The truth was, one of the reasons he ran for mayor in the first place was to assure the hotel was destroyed. And if his company could benefit from a new golf course, even better.

"Mayor Fox, would you like to help?" Amelia held out her rake.

"No, not today," he answered, thinking, *Not any day.* She returned to raking.

"Build the skatepark, Mayor!" Chase called again, climbing the oak tree after Hunter.

"Chase, Hunter! Get down from that tree!" Mr. Kelly shouted. The boys jumped down.

Ryan grinned at Matt, who returned a weak smile. Ryan looked up to the window. Matt followed his gaze. A wavy gray shadow and a golden flicker of light shimmered for an instant, then vanished.

Ryan chuckled. "I'll see you at the council meeting, Mayor."

Matt removed his cap and wiped the sweat from his forehead. "Yes, you will, and I hope you're ready for a fight."

"May the best plan win," Ryan replied.

GHOSTS OF AUTUMN

9.
THE POETRY BOOK

The hotel's surroundings looked more welcoming by the end of the workday. Leaves and trash had been cleared, bushes were trimmed, and trees ablaze with autumn color encircled the now cleared grounds. As promised, Mr. Kelly grilled hot dogs for the volunteers, even those who didn't work too hard, namely Chase and Hunter. The rummage sale was scheduled for the following weekend, and the workers were excited and hopeful it would bring in enough money to persuade the city council not to tear the hotel down.

Amelia, Zoey, and TJ carried the last of the garden tools to Mr. Kelly's car and waved goodbye.

"I have an idea," TJ said quietly, drawing the girls closer. "Before we go home, let's go back to the hotel and just explore a little!"

"Let's do it!" Zoey replied.

Sophia, Chase, and Hunter met them on the path.

"Why are you slackers still here?" Hunter asked.

"Wait, you're calling *us* slackers?" TJ replied.

"Yeah," Hunter said, leaning in and squaring his shoulders. "Slacker."

TJ rolled his eyes. "We're going back to the hotel to have a look around. You can come if you want."

"I will!" Sophia smiled at TJ.

Hunter looked to Chase. "Nah, we've been here long enough. It's boring. Besides, I think I hear a PlayStation calling our names." Hunter stretched out his neck, ear forward, listening for the video game. He wasn't the sharpest tool in the box, but despite his annoying habits—talking too much, laughing too loud, and mouth-breathing—he had been a loyal friend to Chase for years. They were like brothers, ride or die.

Without the buzz of people, the hotel seemed darker and almost somber. The boarded windows gave the impression that something inside was too terrible to see.

"Maybe we can find a way in!" Zoey said, her eyes filled with excitement.

"We can try the door," TJ suggested. They crept up the rickety porch steps. "Here goes nothing!" It was locked up tight.

"Maybe the back door?" Sophia suggested. They rounded the building, jiggling boarded windows along the way, each a disappointment.

Circling back, Amelia squinted and pointed up. "What about up there? That window? Most of the glass is busted out. If we can get to the balcony, we can get in."

TJ gazed up through the branches of the oak tree. "We'll have to climb this massive monster."

"Aw, that's a piece of cake!" Zoey chuckled. They watched as she easily shimmied up. "Come on, guys!" she waved. "It's safe enough!"

Amelia, Sophia, and TJ followed. They crossed the sagging balcony and twisted through the window, their eyes darting to every corner of the room.

"Holy moly, this is crazy!" Zoey said under her breath.

"Yeah, we're actually in," Amelia exclaimed, "and no ghosts yet!"

"Oh, wow!" TJ cried. "Look at this organ!"

"Maybe it's the one that plays on its own!" Zoey added.

"My battery's dead!" Sophia cried, looking down at her phone. "I need to take some pics!"

Zoey pulled out the organ bench and sat down. "Let's see if it works. I mean, if it plays on its own it must work, right?" She grinned then pushed down on the silent keys.

"Here, scoot over," Sophia said and sat beside her. "My grandmother has an antique organ like this, and she taught me how it works." She placed her feet on the pedals. "It's called a pump organ. You have to pump the pedals up and down, like riding a bike. When you do, air flows into the bellows, which are like lungs. It's the air pushing through that makes the sound."

Sophia moved her feet and, when she had the rhythm, pushed the keys. An eruption of sound spilled from the organ.

Zoey covered her ears. "If there were ghosts here, they'd be scared away by that!"

"Right?" TJ laughed. "Should we go downstairs?"

They peeked into each room, then descended the stairs. Thin slivers of light revealed the lobby desk below, and, as their eyes adjusted, a coat rack materialized in the corner, appearing to stand guard over the room.

Moving as one, they paused at the entrance to a larger room where old tables and chairs were strewn about.

"This looks like a dining room," Sophia said.

"Big Bob probably ate his last meal here," Zoey added, "before he had a hundred- and sixty-five-dollar bath!"

Amelia made a beeline across the room. A light, not from any window, illuminated an old steamer trunk previously hidden in the shadows. They were spellbound, but not afraid, for there appeared to be nothing sinister about it. Amelia reached her hand through the light and opened the trunk. Inside were dozens of ancient, musty-smelling books, packed in an orderly fashion. The light faded away.

"Okay, that light was weird!" Zoey exclaimed, pulling a book from the trunk. She opened the front cover. "Ew, this is even weirder! Inside it says, 'To my darling, Rose. My heart belongs to you!' So gross!"

TJ chuckled. "Revolting! This one says, 'To Malcolm from Fred.' Fred? Malcolm? I thought Theodore was bad!"

"Isn't it strange to think someone might be reading through our books in a hundred years?" Sophia asked.

"More like our texts and TikToks," TJ grinned. She smiled back, tipping her head slightly. Amelia and Zoey glanced at each other, raising their eyebrows.

Amelia pulled out several volumes, then spotted a large book buried deep in the trunk. Something inside prevented the cover from fully closing. She sat cross-legged and rested it on her lap. Inside, a small brown book was wedged between the pages. The title was so worn she could barely make out the words *Pocket Book of Poetry*, written by an author whose name had long since worn away. Inside was an inscription.

"Oh, wow, you guys are not going to believe this!" They moved closer.

To Bob Thornton,

Come home to me soon!

Love, Jenny

Boston, 1849

"This book belonged to Big Bob!"

Zoey furrowed her brow. "But who was Jenny?"

Amelia flipped through the delicate book then stopped on the back page, where she found a handwritten poem. As she struggled to read the faded words, a thundering noise, strong enough to shake the walls, filled the room. They flew down the stairs to the entry door. Amelia lifted the latch lock as TJ yanked the door open. Spilling out, they ran as fast as they could.

Chase and Hunter watched them from the window upstairs.

"That was awesome!" Hunter exclaimed, fist bumping Chase.

"Dumb little runts," Chase replied. Feeling proud of their accomplishment, they laughed all the way home.

Two ghosts watched them from the window above.

"If those boys can scare the others away," Jenny said to Bob, "we don't stand a chance!"

"Don't you worry," Bob reassured her, "if they come back, I'll take care of 'em. And that's a promise."

Jenny laid her head against his arm, hoping the boys would never return.

54

10.
THE CLUES

The following afternoon, Zoey, Amelia, and TJ lay on the grass in front of Amelia's house, gazing up at the clouds.

Sophia joined them. "What's up?" she asked.

"The hotel is what's up!" Zoey answered, sitting up. "What *was* that yesterday?"

"Oh, don't be too freaked out." Sophia rolled her eyes. "It was just Chase and Hunter. They snuck inside to scare us."

"Buttheads," Zoey replied and lay back down.

"I know! When they came back to the house, they couldn't stop laughing and rubbing it in."

"Well, at least we know it was them and not real ghosts," Amelia countered. "And knowing *that* might actually help us. I have something to show you." She reached into her back pocket and pulled out Bob's poetry book.

"Remember this?"

"Yeah, before we were so rudely interrupted!" Zoey replied.

"Well, there's a handwritten poem in the back. Very faded, but I can still read it."

Finding You

While sitting in this lonely place,
my thoughts are just for you.
I write upon this empty space
my golden dreams anew.
The light shines bright from this tall chest
and lightens all my cares.
I pledge to you my faithful heart
and all my earthly wares.
The morning hour breaks through the day
and sleep falls from my eyes.
I'll wait for you throughout all time
as tuneful chimes arise.
The moments when I pause and dream
will find me sitting here,
recalling when we chased our dreams
and songs were sung so clear.
The sound of your sweet calling
is music to my ears.
I've found a heart of purest gold
to last all through our years.

They all sat up. "Do you think Big Bob wrote that?" TJ asked.
"Who else? If the poetry book was in the hotel all those years
and it was wedged inside another book at the bottom of a trunk,
who else could've written it? And there's more."

She flipped through. "Here, among the printed poems," she pointed, "he wrote the word *desk* and then, a few pages later, *chest*. He also wrote *clock* and *bench* further on. And I don't know if this is important or not, but there are a bunch of pages with the bottom corner torn off, and those are the same ones where just one word is written. Only on those pages."

"Could they be, like, clues?" Sophia asked.

TJ swept his hair to the side. "Well, we know Bob's gold was never found." The girls nodded. "Maybe these are clues to the gold!"

Sophia turned to Amelia. "Can you read the poem again?" Amelia reread it, slower this time.

"There are verbs in the poem: *write, shine, arise, sitting*. There are also individual words, nouns: *desk, chest, clock, bench*," Amelia said. "They could be connected. *Write* and *desk*, *clock* and *arise*, *bench* and *sitting*....the verbs describing the nouns."

"This is like a flippin' English class!" Zoey replied.

"Let's just start by looking for the objects, which means going back to the hotel," Amelia said. "Is everyone down for that?"

"We could volunteer at the rummage sale this Saturday," Sophia suggested. "Then check it out again after everyone leaves, like before."

"That's a good plan," Zoey said, adding, "but leave Chase and Hunter at home this time, capeesh?"

Sophia was fed up with their tricks. "I'll do my best."

GHOSTS OF AUTUMN

11.

FOLLOW WHERE
IT LEADS

The streets lining the park were full, and throngs of people headed straight for the shade structure where the rummage sale was underway. With the heat on to destroy the hotel, members of the preservation society dug deeper to volunteer, donate, and brainstorm ways to protect it. Judging by the crowd at the rummage sale, the cause had become very popular.

Ryan was pleased with the turnout and hoped they'd raise enough for the first stage of renovation to begin. The proposed golf course would soon be put to a vote, and the future of the hotel was hinging on the proceeds from the sale.

Zoey and Amelia worked side-by-side, bagging items at the checkout, while TJ and Sophia playfully hung out at the tables, straightening up and replacing sold items with more donated goods.

Chase and Hunter remembered the rummage sale and called their friends to join in. None of them were interested in helping out or shopping, of course. Hanging out at the ice cream cart and taunting Sophia and her friends was more to their liking.

After the fun of scaring them before, Chase and Hunter were hopeful the four would return to the hotel after the volunteer picnic was over. This time, they had kept everything from Sophia to make her and the others believe the hotel was haunted. With all the wild rumors swirling about, they thought organ music would be just the thing to send them running this time.

When the sale ended, TJ, Amelia, Zoey, and Sophia joined the other volunteers for the picnic on the hotel grounds. Chase and Hunter said their goodbyes and appeared to be headed home, but circled back and hid among the overgrown trees, waiting.

Zoey, Amelia, Sophia, and TJ perched on the sagging steps of the hotel to plan their next move. "Okay," Amelia said, opening the book, "let's start with the first stanza."

While sitting in this lonely place
my thoughts are just for you.
I write upon this empty space
my golden dreams anew.'

She flipped to the first ripped page she could find. "And the first word written is *desk*."

"Call me crazy," Zoey said, "but I think we might be looking for a desk?"

"I think you might be right and, yes, you're a little crazy." Sophia laughed. She opened the camera on her phone. "Everyone's almost gone. Let's see if we can get in."

"Sweet," Chase whispered. "They're going in!" They ran through the overgrowth to the back side of the hotel and found an unlocked door.

The front door was also unlocked. Apparently, no one had checked it. The friends entered without being noticed and, after their eyes adjusted, walked down the hall to the lobby. Only the tall reception desk loomed in the dim room, not a place Bob would have written anything except his name on a ledger. Sophia snapped pictures as they continued on to the dining room.

Stepping over books still scattered about from last time, they searched every cupboard and eyed each piece of furniture. No desk. They moved to the saloon. Still nothing.

"Upstairs?" TJ asked. The girls followed.

The first room was completely empty. But the next one contained several furnishings, including the organ.

Something in the opposite corner caught Sophia's attention. "Hey, that's a desk!" she cried, flying across the room.

"Really?" Zoey looked puzzled. "That doesn't look like any desk I've ever seen."

"Yeah, it's a roll-top desk! You can open and close it, even lock it if you have a special key. Look!" She rolled up the wood tambour covering to reveal a writing space with three tiny drawers nestled inside.

"Ooh, let's have a look!" Amelia eagerly inspected each one. "Nothing," she sighed. "If only we knew *exactly* what we're looking for!"

"Maybe there's something underneath," TJ suggested. Sophia and TJ lifted the desk and laid it down on its side. Spiders spilled out and scurried away.

"Yikes!" Zoey jumped. "Spiders are *no bueno*! There better not be snakes! I'm leaving if there's snakes!"

"Maybe this isn't *the* desk," Sophia suggested. "There could be another one somewhere."

"Could be," Amelia replied, still examining the desk. She removed the drawers again and reached her hand inside the first empty space and then the second.

"Fingers crossed," she said and reached down into the third space. A slow grin appeared across her face as she pulled out a tiny red bundle, tied with twine. Sophia wasted no time snapping a picture. Their excitement was palpable!

"Open it, open it, OPEN IT!" Zoey squealed.

Amelia untied the twine and peeled back the fabric. Inside was a pea-sized gold nugget.

"No way," TJ said under his breath. "Let's see if it's real?" He bit the nugget and showed them the dent in the soft metal.

"It's real!" Zoey cried.

"Wait, there's something else," Sophia said, looking closer. A tiny, yellow piece of paper was nestled beneath the space where the nugget had been. She carefully pulled it out and placed it on her palm, taking a picture with her free hand.

Amelia opened the poetry book to the page with the first missing corner. Holding it to Sophia's palm confirmed it was a perfect match!

"Oh em gee!" Zoey cried. Amelia's hand covered her open mouth.

"Guys," Sophia said, zooming in on her phone, "this corner hasn't yellowed from age. I think it's covered in gold dust!" Using burst mode, she captured a series of photos.

"I think it's safe to say this book *is* full of clues!" TJ exclaimed.

"Hopefully, clues to more gold!" Zoey cried. She looked up and threw her arms to the sky. "Thank you, Bob Thornton!"

A drizzle broke through the window. Thunder clapped. "Sounds like a downpour," TJ said. He looked out the window. "They're almost done cleaning up outside."

"Let's go," Amelia replied, tucking the book and red bundle inside her pocket.

From the next room, Chase and Hunter held their ears to the wall, trying to make sense of the muffled conversation on the other side.

"Maybe we should go?" Hunter whispered. "The rain's coming down."

"Patience, my friend," Chase replied, holding his finger to his mouth. "*Shh.*"

When the voices in the next room got quiet, Chase pointed to Hunter's phone and flashed a thumbs up. Hunter pushed *play*, and music blasted from the Bluetooth speakers he'd hidden beneath the organ. Amelia, Zoey, Sophia, and TJ streamed down the stairs, heading swiftly for the door!

Hunter belly-laughed from the upstairs window. "Dumb little runts! They'll never come here again!" He didn't notice Sophia pausing to take a selfie with the hotel in the background.

"Let's grab the speakers and go," Chase said.

"We got 'em so good!" Hunter boasted, following Chase to the next room.

Both boys perceived a strange stillness in the room. It felt too quiet.

"This room is creepy," Hunter said. "And it's cold!"

The door to the room slammed shut. Dirt, leaves, and rain swirled in through the broken window.

Hunter shouted above the sound of wind, "Am I trippin'? Did the door just slam shut?"

Chase held the speakers. "Or did you just slam the door? Are you trying to scare *me* now?

"No!"

The boys locked eyes. "You better not be messin' with me, Hunter." He turned to leave, but fell, as if he was pushed to the ground.

Chase jumped up. "Hunter, I swear, did you just push me?"

"I didn't do anything!" Hunter retorted. He offered Chase a hand, but Chase just swatted it away.

"Okay, fine!" Hunter headed for the door but was yanked back by his shirt collar. He stumbled to regain his balance.

"Why'd you do that, bruh?" He glared at Chase.

"What are you talking about?" Chase yelled. "I did *nothing*! Help me open this!"

Grabbing the doorknob together, they twisted and pulled, then pulled some more. The door was stuck and resisted all movement. When they paused and let go for a moment, the door swung open, knocking them both to the floor. Horrified, they bounded down the stairs and out the front entrance, not looking back long enough to witness it slamming shut behind them.

Jenny and Bob laughed at the sight of the boys running for their lives.

"Let's hope that's the end of that!" Jenny said.

"We'll see," Bob winked. "Those kids don't learn easily. And seeing how these little sound boxes are still here..." He looked down at the speakers in his hands. "I have a feeling they'll be back."

12.
Speak Up

Mayor Matt Fox and the council were seated. The town hall was filled to capacity, and many attendees were holding up signs. "Preserve the Elk Grove Hotel!" "Don't Destroy Our History!"

Hunter and Chase were there, leaning against the back wall. Chase held a sign that said, "Forget the golf course! Build a skatepark!" while Hunter's was more rudimentary. In large red letters he had written, "There's ghosts in that hotel!"

"Such doofuses," Sophia said, rolling her eyes. "My parents are not gonna be happy when they see his sign."

Zoey anxiously looked over the gathering crowd. "Oh no, it's getting more *peopley* in here."

"Don't worry," Amelia reassured her. "You'll be great! Really." Zoey didn't look convinced. Mr. Kelly wished her luck, adding that he was certain she wouldn't need it.

Mayor Fox pounded the gavel and called the meeting to order. "Welcome, everyone. Please be seated." He waited for the room to settle. "As you all know, we're here tonight to discuss the proposal to raze the Elk Grove Hotel for the purpose of selling the land it stands on, which is necessary for the golf course to go forward. There is an interested buyer waiting. This meeting is for anyone who wants to speak up either for or against."

He scanned the room, his eyes landing on Ryan Kelly. Ryan gave a quick wave and smiled as though they were still friends, which visibly unnerved Matt.

"So, with that…" He hesitated. "Let's get down to business. The floor is now open. Anyone wishing to speak may proceed to the podium."

A line formed as speakers scurried toward the front of the room. Mr. Kelly signaled Zoey to join him. Several citizens spoke on behalf of the golf course, but Ryan was the first to speak in support of the hotel. He stepped up to the podium and opened his notebook. Zoey waited nervously behind him.

"Thank you, Mayor." He nodded to Matt, who returned an icy stare. "My name's Ryan Kelly, and I'm a history teacher at Pioneer Jr. High. I grew up here and have lived here all my life. In addition, I'm the newly elected president of the Historical Society of Elk Grove."

There was applause from supporters. He spoke about the importance of the hotel as a stop along the historic Monterey Trail, linking the gold fields to Sutter's Fort to the embarcadero. He told about the Hall family and their contribution to the town. He made the case for the hotel to be made into a museum of gold rush history. He left no stone unturned. He got dramatic in his closing segment.

"The hotel *is* Elk Grove. It all started there. If it's torn down, we can *never* get it back! And I believe current and future citizens of this town deserve to have this landmark preserved and restored. In addition, the historical society has been working hard to raise the necessary funds. Please consider carefully and vote to save the Elk Grove Hotel. Thank you."

"Your turn, kiddo!" he whispered to Zoey before returning to his seat. Zoey timidly approached the podium, but before she could speak, an angry woman jumped up and shouted at the council.

"Be honest, Mayor!" she yelled. "Do we really have a say in this decision, or is it a foregone conclusion?" The crowd grew restless.

"It's all about money!" shouted a gray-haired man, who pointed at Matt. He stood slowly, leaning on his cane. "There's been talk of this for years, so why now? To line your pockets nicely, eh, Mayor? Maybe give your construction company a boost?" He sat down, angrily shaking his head. The room got suddenly very loud in a collective outburst from the attendees.

Matt pounded the gavel and ignored their comments and questions. "Next speaker, please."

Zoey took a deep breath. "Thank you, Mayor Fox and council members." She cleared her throat. "My name is Zoey, and I'm a student at Pioneer Jr. High."

Matt folded his arms and slumped back in his chair.

"There are several reasons why I believe the Elk Grove Hotel should not be torn down to make room for a public golf course. First, the hotel is a historical site, a gold rush landmark, that has been in our community for as long as it has been a community. Why not turn it into a museum to teach people the history of our town?" Matt glared at Ryan. "Wouldn't that make more sense than building a golf course?"

Zoey stopped, folded her paper, and looked to the council. She began speaking from her heart. "Mayor Fox, the hotel is special. Please don't tear it down. Too many old buildings are torn down to make way for new things. They aren't better, just newer. The hotel can teach us about our history in a way reading a textbook can't. The Hall family was brave. They risked their lives to come here. The hotel was their dream. They even named the town! It's important for us, and for the people of the future, to experience it. It's a place Elk Grove can be proud of. Thank you."

Amelia, Sophia, and TJ stood and, along with many others, gave Zoey a standing ovation. The room was filled with applause. Mr. Kelly was beaming. Even Zoey was pleasantly surprised at how well she had done.

Next up, a woman bearing a strong resemblance to Sophia approached the microphone. "Oh no, it's my mom," Sophia whispered, sinking down in her chair. "I didn't know she was gonna go up there." She pulled up her hood.

"Thank you, Mayor and council. I am here to speak on behalf of the golf course." Her voice was firm. "The hotel has been lifeless and uninhabitable for decades. We all know and appreciate that it was part of the town's history, but we must admit, the hotel could have been restored many times over by now. It just sits there! Let's make this happen now. The golf course will be a place for everyone to enjoy!"

Sophia looked mortified. Amelia reached over and took her hand. "I used to agree with my parents," she whispered, "but I don't anymore." Amelia nodded and squeezed her hand. Sophia smiled at her, gratefully.

Many others approached the podium that night. When the last person had spoken, the mayor stood to give his opinion.

"I'm sure many of you are aware that the police department has done its best to patrol the undeveloped area of the park where the hotel is located. It's extremely difficult because there's not an actual road there, only a walking path. Unfortunately, there have been trespassers who, on several occasions, have been able to break in." The four glanced over at each other. He went on. "The hotel's foundation is very unsafe, and it's also a fire hazard." He made an attempt to look and sound upbeat. "A golf course would be a great boon to the community!"

Mr. Kelly stood and called out, "But, Mayor!" The room exploded in angry shouts.

Matt ignored Ryan and spoke up above the loud boos. "Two weeks from tonight, we will announce the final plan. This meeting is adjourned."

Matt pounded the gavel and raced out the back door before anyone could stop him. He set his jaw and his resolve even more firm. The hotel had to go!

Then, reflecting on the money his construction company was going to make, he decided it was well worth the irritation.

13.
DID SOMEONE SAY PARTY?

"Hey guys, did you get my text about the Halloween party?" Sophia asked, catching up to the others. The final bell rang, and they headed out the school gate, ready for the weekend to begin.

"Sure did," Zoey answered. "Can't wait!"

"A Halloween party will be sweet!" TJ added. "I haven't been to one since fourth grade!"

"I wish we would have been better friends back then," Sophia said wistfully.

"But there's no time like the present," Zoey replied, "and your party will be the coolest!"

Sophia cheered up. "Costumes, tons of food, good music, even trick-or-treating at the end."

"Sounds super-awesome!" Amelia replied. "Maybe I'll be Sherlock Holmes. Anyone want to be Watson?"

"Elementary, my dear," Zoey laughed, then looked puzzled. "Wait. I think Sherlock's supposed to say that?"

"Speaking of detectives," TJ cut in, "tomorrow's our big return to the hotel."

"My brother and Hunter will be at the skating rink in the afternoon. We should go while they're gone."

"Perfect," TJ replied.

Amelia pulled out the poetry book. She read the next clue out loud.

The light shines bright from this tall chest
And lightens all my cares.
I pledge to you my loving heart
and all my earthly wares.

And the second ripped page had the word *chest* scrawled on it.

"Maybe a tall chest?" Zoey asked. "Hm, like a dresser? With drawers?"

"Could be," TJ answered. "At least that's a good place to start."

Chase and Hunter rounded the corner on their skateboards and jumped off in front of them. "Hey dweebs, what's up?" Chase looked at TJ and his sister and smirked. "You planning on going back to the hotel anytime soon?"

"What's it to you?" TJ replied.

"What's it to *us*?" Hunter repeated, rubbing his chin. "Let's see...last time I checked, you were all running from the hotel, TJ. Something must have scared you."

"I don't recall anything scaring us," TJ lied.

"Just your ugly face in my selfie!" Sophia replied, holding her phone out to him.

"Listen," Chase said, focusing on his sister, "stay away from the hotel, Sophia. It's not safe. You hear me? It's *not* safe!"

Sophia was taken aback by her brother's serious tone, but also determined not to fall for his tricks again. "I don't believe you." TJ put his arm around her shoulder.

"Oh, I see how it is," Chase scoffed. "Your boyfriend's gonna protect you, huh?" Chase and Hunter laughed a little too loud.

"You're worried about *our* safety, Chase?" Amelia cried. "You're a hypocrite! You didn't care when you pulled that stupid prank before. Why are you worried now? Just leave us alone!"

"There's ghosts in there, little girlie," Hunter chuckled, putting his face close to Amelia's. "They're gonna getcha if you go back." He turned to Sophia. "And your boyfriend won't be able to do nothin' to protect you."

"Knock it off, Hunter," Chase said, turning to his sister. "I mean it, Sophia. It's not safe there." He surprised her with a quick hug, and they skated away.

"Well, then," Amelia said defiantly, "what do you say we make our way to the hotel tomorrow afternoon?"

"Oh, yeah." Sophia looked determined. "I'm *so* there."

GHOSTS OF AUTUMN

74

14.
A GAME OF CLUES

"We could split up and go for more than one clue," TJ suggested.

"Great!" Amelia read the next clue.

The morning hour breaks through the day
and sleep falls from my eyes.

I'll wait for you throughout all time
as tuneful chimes arise.

Sophia repeated, "Morning hour and tuneful chimes."

"The next single word is *clock*," Amelia added. "So, a clock that chimes? Or, at least, chimed back then?"

"A mantle clock or a grandfather clock, maybe?" Zoey said.

"Could be," TJ replied. "I know it's a long shot, but what's the next clue?"

"The moments when I pause and dream will find me sitting here, recalling when we chased our dreams and songs were sung so clear.'

"And the single word is *bench*."

"So, let's split up and look for a chest, a clock, and a bench of some sort," TJ said, ticking the objects off on his fingers. Sophia pulled out her phone and tapped on the camera.

They walked through the dusky hallway. Pencil-thin slivers of overcast light streamed in, but they were barely able to see. The wind slammed the door behind them.

"I'll go upstairs," Amelia said, "and start looking for the chest."

"I'll go with you," Zoey replied, looking over her shoulder as they climbed.

Sophia and TJ searched the dining room downstairs. She took photos of the trunk and books still scattered on the ground from last time. They moved on to the next room.

The saloon was much smaller and, having no windows, darker than the dining room. Sophia opened her phone flashlight. Wooden barstools and worn chairs were stacked high atop the bar and poker tables.

"No clock," Sophia said, clicking photos. "So now what?"

While considering their next move, flickers of light appeared in the far corner, hovering above two trunks, one blue leather, the other brown canvas.

"I think the lights are leading us!" TJ said.

They side-glanced each other, then scrambled to open the latches. Inside the brown trunk were hotel registers and some disorganized papers. TJ rifled through it until something caught his eye. He stuffed a paper into the pocket of his jacket.

"TJ, look!" Sophia exclaimed, capturing more pictures. He turned to see Sophia pull a long blue dress from the blue trunk.

Upstairs, Amelia and Zoey searched the ballroom for a chest.

"Ugh, how will we ever find *anything* in here?" Amelia exclaimed. "There's so much stuff!"

"Yeah, it's a mess," Zoey replied, "but we gotta try."

She set about dismantling the pile of furniture stacked along the wall. Amelia dug in to help. They moved chair after chair and table after table, but there was not a chest, bureau, or cabinet of any kind. Disappointed, they took a break and sat on the floor, staring at the disarray.

"Well, the gold isn't gonna find itself," Zoey finally said, lifting herself up. She noticed a light glowing above a tall piece of furniture, still buried.

"Do you see what I see?" Amelia asked, not taking her eyes off the light.

"Yeah," Zoey replied, "but where's it coming from? The sun isn't out!" Amelia shrugged.

They unburied it and, once it was revealed, the light was gone, and the room was gray once again.

"Is it possible?" Amelia asked.

Zoey patted the chest. "It just might be! Let's have a look inside this baby." Amelia jimmied the drawers open, handing each one to Zoey to inspect.

"Nothing," Zoey shrugged. "I don't get it! And what's with the weird light?!"

"Right?" Amelia agreed. "We should look underneath, but it's too heavy to lift." She paused to consider. "Maybe we can shake it a little."

They rocked the chest back and forth, which produced nothing but displaced spiders, until a small red parcel fell to the floor. Zoey shrieked and snatched it up.

Inside was another gold nugget and a torn paper corner.

Downstairs, Sophia held up the dress, imagining the woman who'd once worn it so many years ago. Still nestled in the trunk were a pair of ladies' black high-button shoes, a bonnet, and white kid gloves. Brushing these and other items aside, Sophia's fingers tapped something solid.

"What the—" she whispered and pulled out a wooden mantle clock.

Upstairs, the girls couldn't wait to share the news of their discovery with Sophia and TJ.

"We found the chest and another gold nugget, same as before!" Amelia exclaimed, rushing down the stairs and into the saloon.

Sophia's eyes were wide. TJ held the clock up for Amelia to see, then opened the latch on the back of the casing.

"It has chimes!" Sophia cried. "And there's something in the corner!"

She gingerly reached her fingers inside and pulled out another red bundle, revealing the third gold nugget and another gold-dusted corner. Amelia turned to share her excitement with Zoey. But she wasn't there.

"Where's Zoey?"

"We haven't seen her," TJ replied.

"Zoey?" she called, running from the room.

They searched each room downstairs, eventually heading up and peeking into each of the upstairs rooms.

TJ touched Sophia's arm. "Wait. I hear something," he whispered, stopping at Room 202.

They held their breath and entered the dark room. They noticed Zoey, curled up in the far corner hugging her legs, her head buried in her knees. Amelia sat beside her and wrapped her arm around Zoey's shoulder.

"What happened?"

Zoey was dazed and trembling. She looked up at Amelia. "We were going downstairs. I heard a noise in here and came to see what it was." Amelia gently pulled a strand of damp hair from Zoey's eye. "There was...a...woman standing beside the organ. A ghostly woman with a bright light shining through her. And the room smelled like roses." They all turned to the organ, which looked undisturbed in the far corner of the room. Sophia captured pictures.

"She pulled out the bench and sat down like she was going to play. I thought she didn't see me. But then a man appeared beside her—a man in red. They turned to me, and he said, 'Keep searching, Zoey. You're almost there.' And just like that, they disappeared, and the light was gone and the smell of roses, too."

Lightning flickered, but they heard no thunder.

"Assuming Bob was the man, who was the woman?" Sophia asked. "And...uh, how'd she know your name?"

Zoey's hands were shaking. "That was the scariest part—knowing my name."

"I don't know," TJ replied, "but I think we should check the organ bench. I have a feeling we're about to find another gold nugget."

A ghostly woman with light shining through her played the organ while a man stood beside her.

15. Could It Be?

"I'll hold onto these," Amelia said, shoving the small parcels into the pocket of her jean jacket, including the most recent nugget found in the organ bench. They huddled together under a playground covering in the park, waiting for the rain to pass.

"Are you okay, Zoey?" Sophia asked.

"Still a bit shaky," she admitted, "but okay. It was weird, but not exactly scary, if that makes any sense."

"I'm scared just hearing about it!" Sophia replied. "You were so brave. I would have run out screaming!" They welcomed a reason to laugh.

"Hey, we've found three gold nuggets," TJ said. "That's something to celebrate!"

"And only one more clue to solve!" Sophia added.

"There's something you haven't seen yet," he said, taking a crumbling and folded paper from his pocket. The name Jenny was written across it. He opened it, pointing out the torn edge.

Amelia put her hand to her mouth. "It's the missing page from the poetry book!"

TJ read it out loud.

9 October 1851
Dear Jenny,

I am staying at the Elk Grove Hotel in Elk Grove, California. I am returning the poetry book for your safekeeping. Read between the lines.

Yours, Bob

"*Read between the lines*?" Amelia cut in. "Bob wrote words between the lines of the poems!"

"Yeah, and there's more," TJ said. He read on.

Mrs. Hall, If something happens to me, please mail this letter along with the poetry book to Jenny Weatherly, 210 Cambridge Street, Boston, Massachusetts.

"The letter was never sent," Sophia said sympathetically. "Jenny never saw the poetry book again!"

"The letter wasn't even *with* the poetry book," TJ replied. "It was in the bottom of an old trunk in the saloon. Mrs. Hall never even saw this note. Somehow the poetry book and the letter were separated."

Zoey was beginning to connect the dots. "The woman at the organ? Was she Jenny?"

"Wait! What was the ghost wearing?" Sophia asked.

"A long blue dress."

Sophia turned to TJ. "TJ, the blue trunk! That was Jenny's trunk! Her blue dress!"

TJ's eyes dropped to the letter. "Jenny was here."

"That means she was here to find Bob and didn't even know about the gold," Amelia added, "But what happened to her? It's very mysterious."

"Did she die here, too?" Zoey asked.

"She must have," TJ finally said. "And you saw Bob *and* Jenny, so, together, they're leading us to the gold!" He carefully refolded the letter and put it in his pocket.

"They told me to keep looking," Zoey replied, "and said we were almost there."

"Judging from the lights that appear and disappear, that's a certainty," Amelia said.

A familiar voice called to them, "Go home and get out of the rain, you little twerps!" Chase yelled.

Sophia rolled her eyes. "Same to both of you!"

"Nah, we got business to attend to," Hunter cried. They walked on in the pouring rain.

"Ya know, I've been thinking." Amelia kept an eye on the boys. "What'll we do with the gold if we find it?"

"When, not if," Zoey chuckled.

"The city council will make their decision soon," TJ cut in. "If they vote to tear down the hotel, they won't waste any time before building the golf course."

"Then we have to find the gold before that happens!" Zoey insisted.

"I have an idea," Sophia said. "After my party, everyone's going trick-or-treating. What if we ditch that and come back here for the final clue?"

"Ditch it, find it, save it," Zoey said. "That works!"

Amelia reading Bob's letter

16.
A Quick Return

"Aw jeez, I can't believe we're doing this!" Hunter grumbled, shuffling up to the front door of the hotel.

"I need my speakers, bruh," Chase replied. "We'll just go in, grab 'em and get out."

Hunter didn't look convinced. "We may not make it out!"

"Oh, don't be so dramatic! It wasn't that bad! We're still alive."

"I don't know, dude," Hunter said, shaking his head. "I don't like this one bit!"

"We're goin' in," Chase demanded.

Hunter reluctantly followed.

The door creaked loudly in protest. Inside the dim hallway, shadows played tricks on their eyes. The stairway loomed ahead, filled with more spiderwebs than they remembered. Batting them away, they continued up. A family of mice squeaked and scurried away.

"Do you smell that?" Hunter asked.

Chase sniffed the air. "Smells like roses."

They peered down the cold and foreboding hallway. A *whoosh* of wind sent a tree branch screeching against the building.

"I think that's a warning, Chase! We aren't welcome here!"

"It's fine!" Chase replied, stopping in the doorway of Room 202.

Hunter followed so closely he ran smack into Chase's back. Stumbling, he somehow managed to keep his balance.

Chase felt a hand on his shoulder. "Knock it off, Hunter!"

"Knock *what* off? I haven't done anything!"

"You touched me! Keep your hands off me!"

"Uh, dude. No, I didn't. That wasn't me." A puff of air touched Hunter's ear. "Something just breathed in my ear!"

"You're imagining things! Let me get the speakers and we'll go." Hunter knew it wasn't his imagination.

Chase bent beside the organ to retrieve the speakers. The room turned dark, even the windows allowed no light inside. The door slammed shut!

"Chase," Hunter cried, "I can't see anything! We gotta get outta here!"

Chase dropped the speakers and they felt their way to the door. They tried to open it again and again, but it defied all movement. From the ceiling, the spirit of a man looked down, his eyes unearthly. The spirit wailed! A ghost woman appeared, laughing unnaturally, her eyes hollow. Chase and Hunter held onto each other and backed away toward the broken window, their only way out.

"Get out of our house!" the spirit man yelled, drawing his face close to theirs. "Never come back!" The ghost pushed them to the floor. They crawled toward the window as rain poured in.

"Never show your faces here again!" the ghost woman screeched.

Chase felt himself lifted and thrown out the window onto the balcony. Hunter was next, and the speakers followed shortly.

They grabbed them and scrambled down the oak tree, not looking back.

"Oh, I'm so happy that's over," Jenny sighed. "I think I'll play something beautiful on the organ, dear."

"Please do," Bob sighed. "I'm plumb worn out!"

"I hope they finally learned their lesson!" Jenny added. "I really don't like scaring the kids like that."

"Well," Bob chuckled, "this time, I think it's safe to say the lesson has been learned!"

Jenny held out her fist. "It seems the kids hit their fists together when they agree on something."

Bob tapped her tiny hand with his giant fist. "I noticed that, too. Maybe it will bring us just the luck we need!"

17.
ALL IN FAVOR

Mayor Fox dashed into the room with an armful of paperwork and his PowerPoint ready to go. He couldn't wait to push the golf course through and wash his hands of the hotel once and for all. He had been wanting this since he was a boy. The fact that Fox Construction would benefit by building the new golf course didn't hurt either.

He set down the items on the table, then looked up and greeted the council members. "Please be seated, everyone. All members are present, so I'll call this meeting of the Elk Grove City Council to order." The council secretary busily scratched the minutes into a notebook.

This was a closed-door meeting, so only the mayor, council members, and invited guests were allowed to attend. Everyone was aware that the prospect of razing the Elk Grove Hotel to make room for a new golf course was a touchy subject for the town. Not everyone on the council could agree either, but the mayor was certain they would change their minds once they saw the presentation he had planned.

"I've invited the project superintendent for the proposed golf course to join us." He tipped his head to a man in the front row. "He will share blueprints, as well as ideas for staffing and maintenance." He inhaled deeply and clapped his hands together. "So, with that, I will turn the meeting over to the superintendent."

The super introduced templates of what the golf course would look like from ground and aerial views. He was a persuasive salesperson; his descriptions were spectacular. "From the very first tee, the rolling fairways, immaculate greens, and tranquil surroundings allow you to enjoy a challenging yet supremely relaxing round of golf." Photo after photo of beautiful, well-kept, emerald landscapes promised an oasis in the heart of Elk Grove. Many council members were obviously smitten with the idea.

When the superintendent had completed his presentation and was excused to leave, the mayor moved that the golf course should be put to a vote.

"Mayor," Councilwoman Smith interrupted, "can there be a discussion first?"

"Yes, of course." He was irritated.

Councilman Lee sat forward. "Mayor, I understand the benefits of a new golf course to the community. But are we sure there's not another location in the park or somewhere else where we could build it without destroying a historical landmark?"

"Councilman Lee," the mayor answered sharply, "we've discussed this over and over! We're talking about prime land that could *finally* be utilized. The hotel just sits there! Nothing has been done to preserve it! And, I might add, it's not technically a historical landmark!"

Councilwoman Smith straightened up and offered her objection. "But it could be! We only need to prove that the building was a significant part of our gold rush history! I can see to it myself!"

"But at what cost?" Mayor Fox raised his voice. "How will the historical society ever find enough money to restore it? The town certainly doesn't have the money!"

"We may not be able to restore it now, but perhaps in the future," Councilman Lee added. "We must consider the children of our community! This would be a great learning opportunity for them."

The mayor was losing patience. "Look, I know you are both dedicated members of the historical society, and you and Ryan Kelly dream about this all the time! But. It's. A. Pipe. Dream!" He punctuated each word. "The hotel is a dump and a safety hazard," he sneered. "Even the police can't keep trespassers out. Give me a break!"

Councilwoman Smith wasn't about to give in. "Matt, I've known you all your life, so I'm gonna ask you to hear me out. Before we take a vote, I'd like everyone to just take a step back. Ask yourselves this question. Would you vote to save the hotel if the money *was* there to preserve it? Dig deep. If the answer is yes, then tearing it down would be a tragic mistake."

"Duly noted, Councilwoman," the mayor responded, stifling a yawn. "Is there any further discussion on the motion to raze the hotel for the purpose of selling the land to build a golf course?" The council was silent.

"Then let it be noted there is no more call for discussion, and we'll proceed to the vote. Those in favor of razing the hotel, say aye." Four ayes were counted. "Those opposed, say no." Only Councilwoman Smith and Councilman Lee responded.

"Let the record show that the proposal to raze the hotel has passed." Councilwoman Smith looked down the table at Councilman Lee and shook her head.

Mayor Fox was giddy. "Now comes the fun part." He grinned. "Breaking the news to the community at our next public meeting. I expect all of you will be there and, in the meantime, please keep this decision to yourselves until after we have publicly communicated the plan."

Then, pounding the gavel, he finalized it. "This meeting is adjourned."

Councilwoman Smith watched the mayor gather his things and exit the room, looking very pleased with himself.

18.
WHATEVER IT TAKES

Matt pressed the key fob to lock his pickup. He strode across the park to the hotel path, a little more spring in his step now that the decision about the hotel had been made. Only the logistics to approve remained, and the demolition would be underway.

He stopped when the hotel came into view. The nightmare of his childhood was about to be annihilated. And once it was gone, his business would grow when the golf course was built. It was a win-win situation—at least for Mayor Fox.

He shielded his eyes and looked up at the broken window. The memory of that day flooded his thoughts. *"Matt, I'm in!"* Ryan had yelled, beaming down. Matt had felt excitement and fear all at the same time, not unlike his current emotions.

Matt stepped up to the entrance, chuckling to himself when he realized it was the first time he'd ever entered through the door. Once inside, he walked to the stairway, remembering it like it was yesterday—Ryan, carefree and happy, barreling down those stairs while he anxiously followed, frightened at every turn.

Matt felt wistful and, he had to admit, a little sad remembering his childhood buddy and all the adventures they had shared. Because of Ryan, Matt had gone places and experienced things he never would have tried on his own. Building rafts to float down the slough, constructing treehouses, and climbing to the roof of the old theater just to watch the stars at night were some of his best childhood memories. But breaking into the old hotel was something else altogether.

Focus, Matt, he reminded himself, and got back to business. He decided an excavator would be necessary to dismantle the top story first. And, oh, how he longed to be the first one behind the wheel of that excavator! The non-load-bearing walls would be next in preparation for the explosives that would cause the hotel to collapse. He didn't care what it would take. The necessary permits would be filed immediately, and he would begin the process of restoring his peace of mind.

Matt stepped onto the porch and pulled the door toward him. He paused for a time, then stepped back inside. He climbed the staircase for one last look upstairs. At the landing, he stared down the long hallway. A wooden sign that said 202, written the old-fashioned way, still hung from a rusty nail above the door. His footsteps echoed as he crossed to the window.

When he saw the organ in the corner, his breath became shallow. He remembered the sound of the organ rolling across the planked floor and found comfort knowing it would soon be destroyed along with the hotel.

A flicker of movement from the grove outside caught his eye. Someone was walking toward the hotel. *Who would be coming here?* he wondered, and as the person drew closer, he recognized him. He had known him well, once upon a time. Matt felt a stab to his heart, recalling the day he'd ended their friendship.

He regretted that decision now. But what was in the past needed to stay there. They were on opposing sides of the issue.

Ryan wanted to save the hotel, and Matt couldn't wait to destroy it. Nothing had changed.

Matt moved back from the window, hoping Ryan wouldn't see him. Hearing the door open below, he put one leg at a time through the window, hoping to hide on the balcony and avoid meeting face-to-face.

Matt attempted to stand but felt the balcony shake. His weight was too much for the balcony to bear. First came a faint rumble and then the balcony started to fall. He grabbed the windowsill just as the balcony crumbled into a pile of rubble below.

"Help!" he yelled, hoping his childhood friend would hear him. "Ryan! Help!" He heard fast footsteps on the stairs. His hands were slipping, He closed his eyes and waited to fall.

But he didn't. Two strong hands took hold of his wrists and pulled him up and through the window to safety. *I'm saved,* he sighed and opened his eyes, expecting to see his old friend. Instead, he saw another familiar face from the past. The man in red stood before him. Alongside him was the woman in blue.

"Thank you," Matt murmured. Bob tipped his hat, and they were gone.

"Hi, Matt," Ryan said from the doorway, grinning. "In case you haven't noticed, they're still here."

"Wh-whatever it takes, Ryan," he stammered. "We…we gotta save this place!"

Ryan agreed. "Yes, Matt, we do!"

Ryan and Matt explore the Elk Grove Hotel, 1990

19.
SHAKE IT OFF

Matt had known all along there was another location where the golf course could be built. And without the need to destroy the hotel first, the alternate location would have been more profitable for him. Money was nice, but it was never the primary motivator. And now that this was no longer a factor, he knew he must change the council's minds again if the hotel had a chance of surviving.

He invited Ryan, as president of the historical society, to attend the emergency meeting he'd called at the last minute.

"I'm just gonna lay it on the line," Matt said, standing outside the hall with Ryan before the meeting began. "The public meeting is soon, and this has to be stopped." He looked nervous.

"You're a persuasive guy, Matt," Ryan said sympathetically. "You can do this."

"I sure hope so," Matt replied.

"I'll help if I can," Ryan added.

The council members marched into the room, not sure why they had been asked to reconvene so soon after the last meeting. Matt joined them at the table, and Ryan took an empty seat behind him.

"I'm sure you're all wondering why we're here," Matt began. He had their rapt attention. "At our last meeting, we voted to raze the Elk Grove Hotel for the purpose of building a new golf course. The vote was 4 to 2, in favor." He couldn't help wringing his hands. "I've had some time to think about this decision. I feel we were too rash and need to think this through more."

The council members were confused. Voices broke out between them. Councilwoman Smith and Councilman Lee locked eyes and stifled their grins.

"Mayor, does this mean the golf course is on hold?" Councilman Lee asked.

"No, Councilman Lee," Matt replied, "it means we may have another option. One that won't include destroying the hotel."

"Where? Is the property in a prime location? Somewhere else in the park?"

Matt aimed to reassure them. "Not in the park, but still a great location."

"But we passed this already!" another council member exclaimed. "Why, Mayor?"

Matt's voice was shaky. "Well, we did, but after much thought, I think we need to revisit that decision. The hotel is historical, and I-I think we should respect the place it has in our history."

"Bravo, Mayor," Councilwoman Smith called out. Councilman Lee clapped.

"The hotel is run down, but it's still salvageable," Matt continued, regaining his composure.

"This is a complete reversal! Where do you propose the money will come from to renovate?" another council member asked. "We simply don't have it!"

Matt looked back at Ryan. Ryan stood. "Forgive me for interrupting. I'm Ryan Kelly, president of the Elk Grove Historical Society."

"Yes, we know you, Mr. Kelly," the councilman added.

Ryan ignored him. "The society has been holding fundraisers, admittedly, for a while now. We get closer to our goal after each one. The funds *will* be forthcoming for a full refurbishment and remodel, which will include a museum of Sacramento County history."

"The operative word is *forthcoming*," the councilman scoffed. "I don't know about the rest of you, but I say no money, no way. The hotel's a decaying mess! There's no point saving it! My vote stands."

"I'm firm on my vote, too!" the councilwoman added.

"Can we at least take a new vote?" Matt asked hoping there'd be a tie.

"No money, no change of vote," the councilman repeated, flat-palming the table.

"Alright," Matt replied, disheartened. His hands were tied. "The vote stands. We'll break it to the public tomorrow night."

"I'd be willing to make a deal with you, Mayor," the councilwoman offered. "If you find enough to fund the museum project before the demolition date, I'll agree to explore another location for the golf course."

"Yeah, like that's gonna happen," the councilman chuckled. "But why not? I'll agree to that, too!" Then he added, "Good luck with that, Mayor."

Matt's face dropped. *What have I done?* The demolition was scheduled to begin in two weeks. There was no way to raise enough money in that time frame. The word *impossible* leapt to mind, but Matt shook it off. He couldn't give up yet. He wouldn't give up.

20.
THE DECISION

Amelia, Zoey, Sophia, and TJ entered the Elk Grove Town Hall and found their seats near Mr. Kelly and some other students from class. The hall was abuzz with discussions about the future of the hotel.

Amelia leaned in closer to Sophia. "How are the party plans going?"

"Great!" she replied. "The hay bales and pumpkins are in the backyard, and we're going shopping after school for more stuff."

Zoey perked up. "I can't wait! How hard do you think it will be to sneak away to the hotel that night?"

"Not that hard. We'll break into groups and since the four of us are always together, I don't think anyone will notice or care."

"Maybe your brother will," TJ replied, "and Hunter."

"We'll just have to outsmart them." She turned to the back of the room. "There they are. My brother keeps warning me about the hotel. Not sure why. I almost think he cares."

"I hope they don't follow us this time," Amelia said. "That would throw everything off."

"Like Sophia said, we'll outsmart them!" Zoey winked. "Oh, and we better wear costumes we can run in, just in case."

"And bring our phones," Amelia reminded them. "We'll for sure need our flashlights."

"Hey, there," Mr. Kelly interrupted, stopping into the aisle next to them. "Looks like you're having a deep discussion. About the hotel, I presume."

"Uh, yeah," TJ responded. "You could say that. The hotel."

"And my Halloween party this weekend," Sophia added.

"Sounds like fun," Mr. Kelly replied. "And now the big news!"

Mayor Fox pounded the gavel. The crowd quieted down, and everyone found a place to sit.

"Good evening, everyone. I know you're all anxious for a decision." He spotted Ryan. "This hasn't been easy. A few days ago, the council voted. The decision was in favor of building the golf course where the hotel now stands." Supporters of the golf course cheered. But the other side drowned them out with angry boos. Disappointment washed over the friends' faces.

The mayor raised his hand to quiet the crowd. "Hold up! There's something else I'd like to say. I'll admit that originally, I voted to raze the hotel for the golf course."

"Should've voted for a skatepark!" Hunter yelled.

Chase elbowed him. "Shut up! Bad timing, bruh." Hunter shrugged.

"But since then, I've had a change of heart. Unfortunately, the proposal was already passed, which sealed the deal, so to speak."

The councilwoman spoke up. "But Mayor, we also made a *deal*, remember?" She was concerned this decision could cost her votes in the upcoming election. "Find the money to restore the hotel before the demolition begins, and we can look at other locations. Supporters of the hotel can pitch in if it's that important to them."

"Impossible!" Matt replied. Worry lines on his face deepened. "That's only two weeks away!"

"Take it or leave it, Mayor," she replied, unfazed. "That was the deal. Let's have faith in the citizens of our community. They'll pitch in, I'm sure!" The crowd was becoming agitated and unruly. Some voices yelled at the council. Matt knew he needed to shut it down.

"I'm sorry. The decision has been made! It's done. Please go home...peacefully." He pounded the gavel, looking physically ill. Ryan put his head down.

"We *have* to find the gold!" Sophia whispered. "We *will* find the gold. And when we do, we'll call their bluff!"

"That's the spirit!" TJ exclaimed.

104

21.
HALLOWEEN NIGHT

"What's the last clue?" TJ asked, riding his skateboard alongside Amelia and Zoey as they walked. They were on their way to Sophia's party. Amelia tossed her long braids back over her tie-dyed shirt, reciting the poem from memory.

The sound of your sweet calling

is music to my ears.

I've found a heart of purest gold

to last all through the years.

Zoey combed through her dark hair with her fingers and re-positioned her black cat headband. "Alright, my clever friends, let's break it down. Was there another single word?"

"No," Amelia answered. "All the final clues we have are in this stanza."

"So, whatever or whoever is calling him is music to his ears," Zoey replied. "And he's found a heart of purest gold to love all through the years."

They rounded the corner. TJ jumped off and picked up his skateboard. All around them, kids in costumes flooded the streets, dashing door to door, holding their bags out for treats.

The porch was ablaze with twinkling orange and purple fairy lights. Jack-o'-lanterns guarded the front door. Droopy spider webs hung from every corner, and a gigantic furry spider waited on a porch swing that swayed in the autumn breeze. Chase and Hunter sat on the steps, handing out candy to younger trick-or-treaters.

Sophia met her friends at the door. "Come quick," she said, leading them to a mud room off the kitchen. "Are we ready to do this?" she asked, closing the door.

"Yes," Zoey said. "We were just going over the final clue."

"Oh, wow!" Sophia was barely able to contain her excitement. "What do you guys think?"

"The clue contains keywords," Amelia said. "*Music, heart,* and *gold.*"

"Sound and music. Sound and music," TJ repeated. "Sound and MUSIC! The organ? Could it be in the organ?"

"Maybe," Zoey mused, "but what about *heart of gold*?"

"The heart is in the chest." TJ bit his bottom lip and stared into space, hoping an answer would come. "Was Bob trying to tell Jenny that the gold was inside the organ? In the *heart* of the organ?"

"Wait," Sophia cut in, "the back of an organ is called a chest. Jenny played the organ! She would have known that!"

"Oh em gee," Zoey said, rubbing the goosebumps on her arms. "The gold is inside the chest of the organ?"

A sharp knock on the door startled them. "Sophia?" Chase called from the other side of the door. "What are you guys doing in there?"

"None of your business!" she answered, opening the door. "We're just talking!" The four friends walked out of the room without an explanation. Zoey flashed him a cheesy grin as she passed by.

Chase narrowed his eyes at TJ. "Stay out of closed places with my sister. Ya hear me?"

"Or what, Chase?" TJ held out his hand for Sophia. She took it, staring at her brother.

Hunter gave Chase a knowing look. "Don't worry, I'll make my point soon," Chase whispered.

Amber lights created a soft glow in the yard. Cornstalks lined the fence and hay bales peppered the lawn. Food tables overflowed with every kind of pizza and candy imaginable. A Halloween playlist was cranked up for dancing. Zoey grabbed Amelia's hand and pulled her out to dance. TJ and Sophia joined, all of them jumping to the base of the music. Chase's eyes were fixed on TJ.

Hunter knew that look. "What are you planning, dude?"

"Just scare him, or worse, embarrass him in front of his girlfriend."

A slower song began to play. Sophia placed her hands on TJ's shoulders, and they swayed to the music.

Zoey cocked her head to the side. "Shall we dance, my dear?"

"Sure! Why not?" Amelia chuckled. The girls awkwardly joined hands and moved from side to side.

"Do you think they'll go back to the hotel before it's a goner?" Hunter asked.

Chase shrugged. "Dunno."

"But what if they do? Would ya follow 'em?"

"Yeah, I would. I definitely would."

"Ya know, we could follow 'em tonight. See where they go. Make sure your sister doesn't go snipe hunting with TJ?"

"Knock it off, Hunter!"

The dance was over. "Let's get some hot cider," Sophia said, leading TJ. She gave her brother a death stare as she passed him. The next thing she knew, TJ was on the ground.

He jumped up. "Chase!" Sophia yelled. "Why'd you do that?"

Chase moved closer, hovering over TJ. "Do what?"

"Why'd you trip me like that?"

"I don't know what you mean, TJ. Bug off."

Sophia saw red. "Chase, stop it! Leave him alone!" She grabbed TJ's arm and left. Amelia and Zoey followed.

"So...we're gonna follow 'em, right?" Hunter grinned, obviously enjoying the drama.

Chase didn't answer. He just stood there, fuming.

22.
LET'S GO!

Chase and Hunter watched from the shadows as Amelia, Sophia, TJ, and Zoey tapped their flashlights on their way to the hotel. A barn owl hooted from a branch high above, its large eyes glowering down, watching. Nocturnal creatures scurried about, heard but unseen. Only the harvest moon lit the sky.

"Let's go!" TJ waved. The door loomed ahead, appearing larger than life. They entered, careful to leave the door open for a quick getaway if necessary.

Chase and Hunter approached the hotel in a stealthy manner and watched the four enter. Through the open door, they could see them ascending the stairway. They crept in behind them, unseen and unheard.

"TJ better watch out," Chase whispered. "If the ghosts don't get him, I will."

Hunter was frightened. "Let's go! It's not worth it!"

"I have to get my sister outta here. I'm not leaving without her."

At the top of the stairs, a door was open. Jenny appeared and waved them in. "It's her!" Zoey grabbed Amelia's arm. They slid sideways past the ghost.

"Sophia!" Chase called from below. Everyone froze.

"Don't answer. Hurry!" she mouthed to TJ. Jenny now floated above the organ, holding a large gold nugget.

TJ pulled out his pocketknife and raced to remove the back cover of the organ chest. They could hear Chase and Hunter clomping up the stairs. Zoey closed the door, hoping to buy time.

"Hurry!" Sophia whispered. TJ's hands moved quickly. The footsteps stopped outside the door. TJ had removed the cover!

Bob materialized in the hallway, his eyes warning Chase and Hunter not to go forward.

"I can't move!" Hunter cried.

Sophia thrust her hand inside, landing on something familiar.

Bob remained, but the spell was broken. "Go easy on your sister, Chase," he said. Then, before he vanished, "Give the kid a break, too." He tipped his hat and was gone. The door to the room swung open.

Sophia needed both hands to pull the bundle from the organ. She laid it down heavily on the floor and they encircled it, waiting for her to untie the twine and peel back the flannel. TJ waved for Chase and Hunter to join them in the circle.

"What is that?" Chase asked.

Sophia turned to her brother. "It's gold! Real gold!" The boys looked confused.

"In the beginning, we were just curious and wanted to have a look around," TJ explained. "But then we found a trunk full of old books, and Amelia discovered a poetry book that had once belonged to a miner named Bob Thornton."

"Mr. Kelly told us about him," Chase remembered. "He was murdered here during the gold rush."

"Yes," Amelia replied. "There were clues in the book and we kept returning, hoping he would lead us to the gold."

"There were five clues," Zoey said, "and tonight we solved the final one that led us to this!" She looked to the numerous, walnut-sized nuggets that glistened in the flashlights.

"It was our very own gold rush!" TJ laughed.

Chase chuckled. "You're okay, kid." Then he pointed. "But you still better be good to my sister, or you'll answer to me." TJ smiled, shyly.

"So, what now?" Hunter asked. "You guys are *rich*!"

"Aww... that's an easy one," Zoey said. "We save the hotel! For Bob and Jenny!"

Chase looked to Hunter, "I bet we know just the person to get it done. In fact, you know him, too."

They contacted Mr. Kelly who wasted no time phoning Mayor Fox.

Bob Thornton, from an 1850 tintype.

23.
BIG NEWS!

The four waited together in the front office of the *Elk Grove Citizen* newspaper. A reporter was scheduled to interview them, and their story would soon appear in the news.

"Should we tell them the whole story?" Zoey asked, biting her thumbnail.

Sophia looked startled. "Everything?"

TJ shrugged. "They wouldn't believe us anyway."

"Yeah," Amelia admitted, "even if it *is* the best story ever!"

Gold! Gold! Gold!

Elk Grove Students Solve 170-Year-Old Mystery
Money to be Donated for the Restoration of the Historic Elk
Grove Hotel and Stage Stop

Below the headline was a black-and-white photo of the four friends smiling for the camera, each showing off an extra-large gold nugget. In the background was their teacher, Mr. Kelly, and Mayor Matt Fox.

The lengthy article explained the controversy surrounding the hotel, as well as the history of the gold that had remained hidden since 1851. News spread fast, and support for the hotel was overwhelming.

The morning after the article appeared, they returned to school as instant celebrities. Mr. Kelly invited them forward for a question-and-answer session.

"Will you keep any of the gold or money from the gold?" a girl asked.

Amelia shook her head. "No, we agreed it should be used for the hotel." Some students groaned.

"Is the hotel a historical landmark now?" a boy in the back wanted to know.

"It will be soon," Sophia replied. "The city council is on it."

The class continued to discuss the adventure until the bell rang and students began filing out the door.

"Hey, TJ, can I talk to you guys for a minute?" Mr. Kelly called. They circled back to their teacher's desk. "I just want you to know how much I appreciate all that you guys have done."

"Yeah, no prob, Mr. K.," TJ replied.

Mr. Kelly appeared to be searching for words. "I was just wondering...when you were at the hotel...I mean, did you see anything out of the ordinary?"

They exchanged looks, not sure what to say. "Just friends, Mr. Kelly," Sophia finally answered. "We only saw friends." She smiled and he understood.

Epilogue

October, One Year Later

"Thanks, everyone, for coming," said Ryan, the new curator of the Elk Grove Museum. He turned the sign in the window to *Closed*.

"It went well, buddy!" Mayor Matt said.

Earlier that morning, Matt had given a moving speech about the hotel's history and then unveiled a plaque, designating the hotel as a historical landmark. Amelia, Zoey, Sophia, and TJ, cheered on by Chase and Hunter, were each presented with a special award for their generous gift. As president of the Elk Grove Historical Society, Ryan received the honor of cutting the ribbon and declaring the museum open to the public.

Photos were taken and Sophia offered to share her photos with local news outlets, who were already competing for rights to the story.

The hotel was beautifully restored. Broken windows had been replaced, and the wood floors were sanded and refinished. New wallpaper, made to match the original, adorned each room. Antique furniture had been repaired and polished for the public to view. The portraits of the Hall family stood out over fresh white paint in the hallway. Outside the hotel was repaired, and a new driveway and parking lot made it easier for the public to access and the police to provide security.

Upstairs, display cases filled the rooms with artifacts and photos. Among these were Mr. Hall's spectacles, Mrs. Hall's yellow apron, hotel ledgers, and articles of tack from the stable that once housed Sally, Bob's mule. Below each item was a brief description and, when known, the name of the previous owner.

Room 202 held the most captivating display of all. There, guests could see a secretary desk, a highboy chest, and a marble-adorned mantle clock. Standing in the corner was the pump organ and, tucked below it, the organ bench. Jenny's floral carpet bag sat on the floor beside a dress form displaying her long, blue dress.

On the sagging antique bed was Bob's hat and what was left of his red shirt. His boots were on the floor below.

Inside a glass case was a pocket-sized poetry book—the very book Jenny had given to Bob when he left Boston and headed for the gold fields of California. The book held the clues to the gold all those years. Beside it was a daguerreotype of the Skinner brothers, found buried in a trunk, the silver in mint condition. The brothers stood side-by-side, expressionless under their hats and holding their pistols close to their hearts. A grim reminder of the hotel's sordid history.

Museum goers gazed at Bob and Jenny's belongings, imagining their lives. What had it been like to travel around Cape Horn on a clipper ship? Did Bob yell, "Gold! Gold! Gold!" when he made his amazing discovery? What had their plans been before their lives were cut short?

Ryan gathered his things and turned off the newly added electric lights. Stopping on the porch, he inspected the recently cleared grove.

"Mr. Kelly!" familiar voices called. He waved enthusiastically to his approaching former students. They had been the first ones to walk through the museum when it opened and were thrilled with the outcome. They couldn't wait to talk it over with him.

"How'd the rest of the day go?" Sophia asked.

Mr. Kelly gave her a thumbs-up. "I think Bob and Jenny would approve! And the town owes you four a debt of gratitude."

"We owe you!" Amelia replied. "We wouldn't have known anything about Bob, Jenny, the Halls...none of it without you!"

He thanked her and turned back to the hotel. "What matters is that the hotel is here, and history lives on."

They chatted about the day and before saying their goodbyes, Sophia insisted on a selfie in front of the hotel.

"Thanks, Mr. K.!" they shouted as he drove away on the newly-paved road, waving out the car's window.

Sophia scrolled through her photos for favorites. She was struck by something that piqued her curiosity. She pinched the screen to look closer.

Zoey noticed. "Sophia, what's going on?"

Not answering, Sophia held up the picture for her to see. In the foreground were five smiling faces. In the background, the hotel was distant and smaller. The windows gleamed, reflecting the sunlight. But when she zoomed in, the figures of Bob and Jenny were clear.

"There's something you don't see every day!" Zoey exclaimed. "A photo of ghosts!"

Sophia looked at her but remained silent. She moved the image and showed it to Zoey again. In the next window, two men grimaced beneath their wide-brimmed hats.

Zoey was horror-struck. "Oh no! It's the Skinner Brothers!"

TO BE CONTINUED...

Fact or Fiction?

The Elk Grove Hotel and Stage Stop

It's a fact that this was a real location, and it is accurately described throughout the story. It was a popular stop on the Monterey Trail, which connected Monterey, the Mexican capitol, to Sutter's Fort and Sutter's Embarcadero.

The building was torn down in 1957 when Highway 99 was built. The Elk Grove Historical Society built a replica, The Elk Grove House and Museum, and it's located in Elk Grove Park.

The Hall Family

It's a fact that in 1840, James and Sarah Hall along with their five children—John, Henry, Anne Adele, and twins Thomas and William—left Liverpool, England, aboard the largest merchant ship of the day, the *Roscius*. According to the passenger list, they reached New York City on October 13, 1840.

The family lived briefly in Wisconsin, Illinois, and Iowa, before joining a wagon train on the Overland Trail heading to California. The gold rush of 1849 was the impetus for their journey. After traveling more than 2,000 miles, the Hall family arrived in Placerville, California, in September 1850. That November, the Halls left Placerville and settled 14 miles south of Sacramento. They built the Elk Grove Hotel and Stage Stop, which was the first building in the area. James named the town Elk Grove.

SHERIFF JOSEPH MCKINNEY

It's a fact that in March 1850, Joseph McKinney became the first elected sheriff in Sacramento County. He held that position for only five months and was killed in the line of duty during the Squatter's Riot of 1850.

Sheriff McKinney died three months before the hotel opened. He is buried at Sutter's Fort Cemetery and honored at the California Peace Officers' memorial at the Sacramento State Capitol.

CYRUS AND GEORGE SKINNER

Cyrus and George were brothers who were considered Old West outlaws. They were involved in the 1856 theft of $80,000 in gold bullion, along with "Rattlesnake" Dick Romero. The theft was unsuccessful when Cyrus and Dick missed the rendezvous location having been captured with stolen mules. George buried half the money before he was killed in the capture. The other half was turned over to the law. George never revealed the location of the other $40,000 in gold, which remains a mystery to this day.

Cyrus and Rattlesnake Dick escaped imprisonment. Cyrus fled to Montana where vigilantes soon tracked him down, held a mock trial, and found him guilty. He was hanged the same night in 1864.

ALL OTHER CHARACTERS AND HAPPENINGS

While the people and locations above are historical, the roles they played in the story are entirely fictional. There is nothing to suggest they ever met, and their experiences come from the author's imagination. For the purpose of the story, dates have been changed to allow personalities to intersect.

The Elk Grove Hotel,
Courtesy of the Elk Grove Historical Society

Cyrus Skinner

James Hall,
the founder of Elk Grove

The Elk Grove House and Museum

Only this drawing of Sheriff Joseph McKinney survives, first sheriff of Sacramento County. Image courtesy of Sacramento County Sheriff's Office

236

Coming soon....
Ghosts of Winter

"Alright, everyone, this concludes our tour. It's time to return to the bus." The students groaned and followed their teacher. Only Tim lingered in the ballroom. He glanced at the four corners where nothing appeared out of the ordinary. Shrugging it off, he followed, too.

Fiddle music began to play. Tim paused then stepped back into the ballroom, his Spidey sense never so sharp. A hazy specter hovered in the corner. It was the ghost of a woman with a gruff demeanor. A grim smirk washed over her nebulous face, black holes where her eyes should be. "There you are, Tim. You have something that belongs to me? Hm?" Her mouth opened unnaturally wide, and she shrieked, "GIVE IT BACK!!!" He stumbled backwards.

The spirit moved closer, now eye-to-eye with Tim. Barely able to breathe, he ran from the room and down the stairs, the last one to board the bus. Abby noticed his sweaty forehead and his shaking hands. "What is it?" she asked. "What happened?" Tim looked at her with wide eyes. He shook his head, pulled the watch from his pocket, and handed it to her.

238

ABOUT THE AUTHOR

Amy Gorder loves to share her fondness for spooky stories intertwined with gold rush history. She was born and raised in the Central Valley of California where ghosts of 1849 loom large. She lives in Elk Grove, California, along with her husband, Chris, and together they have four children and ten grandchildren. As a mother, grandmother, and former elementary school teacher, she has learned that nothing grabs a child's attention faster than a spooky ghost adventure. And if history is learned along the way, all the better. *Ghosts of Autumn* is her first children's book.

GHOSTS OF AUTUMN

ACKNOWLEDGEMENTS

Thanks to my publishing team at Emerald Books. To Jessica Hammerman for her patience, encouragement, and professional skills. To Isaac Peterson for his ability to see the bigger picture and his artwork that brought the words to life. And to Michele Barard for her marketing expertise that sent this story out into the world. I'm so grateful for this wonderful team.

Special thanks, also, to the Elk Grove Historical Society for preserving the past for future generations to learn and enjoy. And to the *Elk Grove Citizen* newspaper for sharing this important archival information with the community.

242